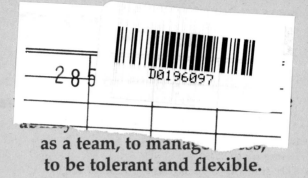

as a team, to manage ____
to be tolerant and flexible.

Flexibility was for the nurses and technologists, not surgeons, but here, he had to adjust.

Instead of heading back toward the nurses' station, Adam headed for the dispensary to carry back a few supplies. He dug into his pocket for the dispensary key, but as he neared the doorway, he saw it was ajar.

Who would leave the room unlocked? He picked up his pace and pushed open the door.

"What are you doing?" he yelled.

A shot tore through him. Heat and pain seared his flesh as his legs buckled.

Books by Gail Gaymer Martin

Steeple Hill Single Title

The Christmas Kite

Love Inspired

Upon a Midnight Clear #117
Secrets of the Heart #147
A Love for Safekeeping #161
Loving Treasures #177
Loving Hearts #199
"The Butterfly Garden"/*Easter Blessings* #202
"All Good Gifts"/*The Harvest* #223
Loving Ways #231
Loving Care #239
Adam's Promise #259

GAIL GAYMER MARTIN

loves life. She cherishes her husband, family, singing, traveling and her Lord. With all those blessings, God gave her one more gift—her dream of writing novels. Gail is multipublished in nonfiction and fiction, with eighteen novels and seven novellas. Her novels have been finalists for numerous awards and have won the Holt Medallion (2001 and 2003), The Texas Winter Rose (2003), the American Christian Romance Writers 2002 Book of the Year Award and a nomination by *Romantic Times* as Best Love Inspired Novel of 2002.

Besides writing, Gail travels across the country guest speaking and presenting writing workshops. She lives in Lathrup Village, Michigan, with Bob—her husband and best friend.

She loves to hear from her readers. Write to her at P.O. Box 760063, Lathrup Village, MI, 48076 and visit her Web site www.gailmartin.com.

ADAM'S PROMISE

GAIL GAYMER MARTIN

Love Inspired.

Published by Steeple Hill Books™

Special thanks and acknowledgment are given to Gail Gaymer Martin
for her contribution to the FAITH ON THE LINE series.

To my editor, Patience Smith, and my agent, Pam Hopkins, for their loving support,
encouragement and direction. I'll never forget their kindness and friendship.

And thanks to surgeons and authors Dr. Mel Hodde and his wife, Cheryl, who write as
Hannah Alexander, and Dr. Harry Kraus, for medical details and advice. To Nancy Williams,
Patty Hall and Carla Long, for answering my nursing questions. To Debbie Kinnard, Spanish
translator, for her assistance. To Lynda Sandoval, aka Lynda Sue Cooper, for answers to my police
and detective questions and, finally to Doris McCraw from the Colorado Springs Visitors Bureau,
for providing me with all the great information.

STEEPLE HILL BOOKS

Steeple
Hill®

ISBN 0-373-87269-0

ADAM'S PROMISE

But the Lord is faithful,
and He will strengthen and protect you
from the evil one.

—2 Thessalonians 3:3

CAST OF CHARACTERS

Dr. Adam Montgomery—After surviving several attempts on his life, the arrogant surgeon has a change in attitude—and in faith.

Katherine Darling—The compassionate nurse offers lots of tender, *loving* care to Adam as he recuperates.

Liza Montgomery—Adam's mother can't resist matchmaking for her eldest son.

Frank Montgomery—The mayor of Colorado Springs is concerned about his injured son as well as the city's rising crime rate.

Dr. Lionel Valenti—Is Adam's co-worker suffering from a mere infection…or something more insidious?

Detective Samuel Vance—Can he stay objective while working on his friend's case?

FAITH ON THE LINE:
Two powerful families wage war on evil…
and find love.

Chapter One

"I don't get it." Kate Darling pivoted her head toward Dr. Adam Montgomery standing in the clinic's office doorway.

"Get what?" Adam pulled his shoulder away from the doorjamb, his stethoscope swaying at his neck as he crossed the room.

Kate gestured toward the papers she held, then used them as a fan. "We ordered adequate supplies last month, but we're running short again. I've checked against our computer records, and it doesn't match. I helped stock the last shipment, and now I'm wondering where my mind is."

"I've wondered that myself," Adam said, standing above her and watching Kate's cheeks tint a soft shade of pink.

Her chair grated against the wooden floor as she shifted and rose to face him. "I'm sorry that you find me inadequate, Dr. Montgomery."

Adam stepped back, surprised at the spunky attitude she'd shown lately. Should he remind her that she was only a nurse? He held back the comment, figuring the hot, humid climate had set them all on edge. "I didn't question your ability as a nurse, Miss Darling. You're an exceptional nurse. I question your competence in keeping accurate records of our supplies."

Her eyes narrowed, and the look she sent him nailed him to the floor. "Perhaps we should hire a local to handle supplies. Is your Spanish prolific enough to give *her* orders?"

Adam held up his hand to calm the waters. "I'm not arguing with you, Katherine. We're dealing with drugs here, and we need to be responsible. We can't lose cartons of morphine and Demerol."

"I didn't lose anything. I just can't find the boxes." She spun around and headed for the doorway.

He watched her rounded hips sway as she charged across the room. Besides being irked by his comment, he knew she hated him to call her Katherine. Everyone called her Kate, but Adam thought that calling her Katherine kept things more professional.

Before she passed through the doorway, Kate paused, eyeing him over her shoulder. "You know, when I volunteered for Doctors Without Borders, I agreed to leave my cozy apartment and come to this village miles from nowhere, except mangroves and jungle." She spun around to face him. "But I didn't agree to be called inadequate." She pivoted again and hurried out of the room.

"Look, Katherine. Come back…please."

In a moment, she reappeared in the threshold, her arms folded across her chest.

"I'm not blaming you. It's a month between shipments, and when we come up short—"

"I know." Kate stepped into the room and approached him, her arms swinging in a hopeless gesture. "I'm upset, too. I don't understand what happened."

A movement at the doorway caught Adam's attention.

"What happened?" The clinic's internist stood inside the doorway, eyeing the two of them. "What's the problem?" Perspiration beaded Lionel Valenti's face, and he pulled out a handkerchief to blot the moisture.

"Our supplies," Kate said, her tone as defeated as she looked.

Valenti's gaze shifted from Kate to Adam as if not sure who had the answer. "What about them?"

"We're running low on some of the meds," Adam said, studying his co-worker's face with concern. The man's haggard look grew worse everyday, and Adam prayed he hadn't contracted some type of jungle virus. The Venezuelan climate had been difficult for everyone.

"I hadn't noticed," Valenti said. "When I give away meds, I list them on the charts."

"No one's accusing anyone," Adam said. "But according to Katherine, the computer records and what's on the shelves don't match."

Valenti shrugged. "Our new shipment should be here on Thursday. It *is* the second Thursday of the month, isn't it? If so, we don't need to worry."

"I'm not worried about running out. I'm worried about being accountable," Adam said.

Kate held up her hand to halt the discussion. "I forgot to tell you. I got a call this morning. The Thursday shipment will arrive on Tuesday, two days early." She shrugged. "Don't ask me why."

Valenti eyed his watch. "Tuesday. July sixth." He swung his arms out at his sides and let them drop. "Then there's no problem. In four days we'll have a restocked dispensary."

"But that still doesn't answer my question," Kate said as she marched toward the doorway and vanished into the hallway.

"What's eating her?" Valenti asked.

Adam shrugged. "Prima donna. She doesn't take criticism well." He swung his frame into the chair Kate had vacated and eyed the computer screen. "She'll get over it."

Valenti leaned over with him and studied the monitor. When he drew back, he swayed and grabbed the chair back to steady himself.

Adam looked into his colleague's face. "I'm concerned about you, Lionel. You don't look well. You're flushed and look tired. Have you checked your temperature?"

"It's nothing," Valenti said, waving Adam's words away. "It's the climate. I hate humidity. And I've got a sinus infection."

"You sure? If you need a day off, we'll cover for you."

"No need. I'm fine." Valenti dug his hands into his lab coat pockets. "We're all looking bad. It's this late shift."

"Someone has to do it," Adam said.

Valenti shrugged. "It doesn't matter. There's not

much to do here anyway except slap at mosquitos and listen to those incessant insects.''

"This isn't Colorado Springs." Adam chuckled. "I have to keep reminding myself this is Santa Maria de Flores. No luxuries here.'' He swiveled the chair from side to side, thinking of the comfortable town house and silver sports car waiting for his return. "I soothe myself with the thought that people wouldn't have medical treatment if we weren't here.''

"You sound like a true humanitarian, Adam.''

Valenti's comment had a sarcastic ring to it, but Adam didn't challenge the man. He'd been tense lately. Like Valenti had said, so had everyone.

Prima donna. Kate stormed away from the doorway with Adam's words ringing in her ears. If she were going to tag someone with that label, *his* name wouldn't be Kate. Daily she struggled to put a Christian spin on Adam's arrogance. He irked her to the core with his Katherine this and Katherine that. Who did he think he was?

Kate's footsteps whispered along the hallway as her thoughts swung from her frustration with Adam to her admiration. The man could be self-centered one minute and filled with compassion the next…when it involved the patients. Beneath her irritation, she admired the man. He'd come from a prestigious family in Colorado Springs. His father was the mayor, and yet, here he was in Venezuela providing health care to the poor in a rustic community so many miles from the comforts of home.

Kate reached the end of the long hallway, turned right for a short distance and entered the dispensary on the left. She scanned the shelves again, concerned. Had she mislabeled the inventory when it arrived? She pulled the ladder to the end of the row and checked the boxes lining the wall.

Perspiration beaded her skin, and with her exertion, moisture collected along her hairline and rolled down her face, stinging her eyes. She blinked and climbed down from the ladder.

Stepping back, she tripped over a pile of empty cartons and gave them a swift kick. A box cartwheeled through the air and landed near the doorway.

"Take that, Adam Montgomery," she said, then chuckled at her childishness.

What made her most angry was her attraction to the man. Since they'd arrived, she'd watched him work and had observed his skill as a plastic surgeon. He transformed deformed children into beautiful youngsters—healthy and unscarred by their tragic births or their horrible mishaps. And, though Adam strutted his stuff in the office, she witnessed a humility when it came to working with the families. His kindness touched her heart. Somewhere beneath that arrogance was a true Christian man.

Longing for a breath of air, Kate turned off the dispensary light, locked the door and walked a step farther to the outside delivery door. Once a month a truck pulled up behind the clinic to bring lifesaving drugs and supplies to the volunteer group of doctors, nurses and personnel who worked there.

Darkness enshrouded her as she stepped outside. No convenient streetlight glowed to dispel the gloom. Only the moon's faint glint flickered from beyond the tree leaves. She stood beside the door, drawing in the humid air. An occasional whiff of breeze rustled the grasses around the stucco building, her home away from home.

Home. She didn't allow herself to think about home. She loved her small apartment in Colorado Springs. She'd made something of herself despite her difficult past, a past she pushed out of her mind as soon as it entered.

Kate peered into the night until her eyesight adjusted to the darkness. In the moonlight, she could see the silhouette of the wild chinaberry and trumpet trees whose dried rose and white flowers still lay crumpled beneath their branches. Despite the remoteness, Kate felt safe surrounded by jungles, lagoons and mangrove swamps.

Feeling comforted by the night, Kate drew in a calming breath and opened the door, returning to her quandary. She passed the dispensary door and treaded the hallway toward the front office. When she turned the corner, she spotted the local woman who cleaned and did odd jobs at the clinic. Kate hurried forward. "*Hola,* Carmen," Kate called.

Carmen stepped backward from an examining room and smiled, her white teeth contrasting her tanned skin. "*¿Sí?*"

Kate slowed her walk and pantomimed as she spoke. "Did you store medicine somewhere besides the dispensary…*la farmacia?*"

"*¿Mi? ¿Medicina?*"

"*Sí.* Did you?"

Carmen's eyes widened. "*No, señorita. No sé nada.*"

I know nothing. Kate peered at the woman, sensing perhaps she did know something.

The young woman's eyes shifted back and forth, and she clutched her hands to her chest.

They had always trusted Carmen. She'd worked for the clinic the past two months, but... Kate cringed at her suspicion. She had no reason or right to accuse this woman without any more proof than a faint inkling. Kate realized she was looking for a scapegoat for her own mistake. Keeping track of the inventory was her responsibility.

"Está bien," Kate said, letting Carmen know everything was fine. She waved her hand in the air as if erasing her earlier question.

A look of relief covered Carmen's concerned face. *"Sí. Gracias."*

Kate forced a halfhearted smile, then continued toward the office. Surprised that she'd let her thoughts wander in such a horrible direction, Kate asked the Lord for forgiveness. Why would Carmen steal the drugs? Kate needed to check the computer again. Perhaps she overlooked something.

But she didn't think so.

Four days later, Adam grasped a moment's reprieve and looked out the small window of his office, watching the sun set behind the wild chinaberry tree. A coconut palm stood tall, unbending in the windless sky. Heat permeated the room, and a pesky jejen—a small voracious fly—circled past, hoping to sink its stinger into his body, Adam figured. He swatted the insect away, then left the office and headed down the hall.

He stopped at an examining room door and checked the clipboard, then walked inside to greet the mother cradling her infant who had received plastic surgery on a cleft palate three weeks earlier.

"Hola," Adam said.

The mother murmured a greeting, not lifting her gaze from her child. Anxiety weighted the woman's expression, and Adam tried to calm her with his limited Spanish.

With the mother standing beside him, he removed the sutures and motioned to the scar. *"Luce bien,"* he said, hoping she agreed that it looked flawless.

She beamed.

As she watched, he demonstrated how to massage the scar in a circular motion, encouraging her to try her hand at the needed therapy. When she finished, he disinfected the site.

"Señora Fernandez, mírame, por favor." He gained her attention and pointed to the dressing, demonstrating how she should change the sterile strips.

The woman nodded, seeming to understand.

Adam lifted the infant and cushioned him in his arm, grateful for the skill God had given him to make a child's life better. Too many children were born with deformities in this land of poverty. Sometimes he wondered how a loving God could allow this to happen, but he'd been raised to trust the Lord and know that all things had a reason.

He turned his thoughts back to the infant and headed to the storage cabinet to locate a supply of plastic strips to give the mother. He knew she would have little money to buy her own.

The cabinet looked almost bare. Why didn't someone see that supplies were in each room?

A rap on the door jarred the thought from his mind. Adam turned, and his pulse skipped. Katherine. Could she read his mind? She stood in the doorway with a pile of sterile strips and bandage supplies clutched in both hands and piled against her chest.

"Sorry to disturb you." A curious look washed over her face as her gaze shifted from him to the baby he held cradled in his arm.

"The supplies just arrived, and I know this room is short," she said. "I imagine you want some of these for Señora Fernandez."

"Thanks," Adam said, puzzled by the coincidence. He returned the infant to his mother while Katherine stocked the cabinet with supplies. Before she left, Katherine handed him several sterile strips.

He slid the bandages into a plastic bag and handed them to Señora Fernandez. Gratefulness filled the woman's face, and her response renewed his sense of purpose.

With the mother content and smiling, Adam guided her to the exit, more for his own need for fresh air than for Señora Fernandez. Adam stood a moment in the dusky light, watching her sandals kick up dust along the side of the road.

Adam rubbed his neck, feeling the strain of what would be a long night's work. He agreed with Valenti. The late shift was difficult.

As he turned, a sting stabbed his arm and looked down in time to see a jejen. He slapped at the fly, but it had already vanished. As he headed inside, Adam's arm stung with a fiery itch, and he rubbed the irritated spot.

When he reached the nurses' station, Kate beckoned to him. She peered at his scratching and grinned. "Got a bite?"

He nodded.

"Vitamin B and baby oil work wonders."

"I know," he said, wanting to remind her he was the physician.

She motioned toward the computer screen. "The supplies are accounted for and stocked. I've checked everything twice."

"Learned your lesson?"

She sent him a fiery look. "You can check it yourself if you'd like." She swung the monitor toward him and rose from the chair.

"I'm joking, Katherine."

Her eyebrows raised as her frown melted. "Well, I just thought…"

He harnessed a chuckle, seeing the look on her face. No one could get as addled as Katherine…at least, when he talked to her. She didn't like him, he figured.

"Do I have another patient?" he asked, needing to get on with his work and not worry about Katherine's fluster.

Kate nodded. "Knife wound. Room two."

Knife wound. He had seen too much of that. Harvesting accidents, street fights and drug- or alcohol-induced arguments. Adam had already seen cuts and bruises from their Independence Day celebration the day before, the fifth of July.

Adam strode into the hallway and headed toward

the examining room. Before he reached the doorway, he felt a hand on his arm that spun him around.

"Look, Montgomery, where do you get off advising my patient to do something I said wasn't necessary?"

Adam felt his jaw drop. "What are you talking about, Dan?" He gazed into Dr. Eckerd's angry eyes.

"I'm talking about Liana Ramirez."

"The child? I don't—"

Eckerd gripped Adam's jacket and crushed the cloth. "Do you remember telling Señora Ramirez that her daughter needed plastic surgery for the birthmark?"

Adam jerked his arm away from the doctor. He faintly remembered one day he'd seen the family in question, but they often shared patients. No one had an exclusive patient list at the clinic. "I recall having the mother ask my advice about the mark. I said that you were correct. Some nevi fade with time, but the girl's is raised and deep purple. It's the type that is often permanent."

"And one that would benefit from plastic surgery."

"Yes, but—"

"This is another example of your cocky attitude and self-importance. You could have discussed it with me first. I think you're wrong. You're costing the clinic money it can't afford and endangering a child's health with your arrogance."

"Dan, my suggestion wasn't arrogance. I based it on my knowledge as a plastic surgeon."

"Next time think about someone else's reputation before you mouth off with your advice."

Adam watched the doctor charge away, and he

stood with his mouth hanging open. What was going on? The climate? The late shift? A full moon? He shook his head and checked the clipboard hanging beside the examining room. Adam recognized the name. He'd seen Felipe Garcia more than once.

"Señor Garcia," Adam said, entering the examining room.

The man gave him a sheepish grin. *"Toma mucho."* He tipped an imaginary bottle and pantomimed taking a drink.

Adam silently agreed he'd had too much alcohol and probably too many drugs. Adam's chest tightened, thinking of the lives destroyed by substance abuse.

In minutes, he'd cleaned and sutured the arm wound. Adam knew the man would have pain and he looked through the cabinet and found the last few tablets of Darvocet. They would do him for now. *"Regrese en de dos días."* He raised two fingers in the air, then pointed downward, indicating he wanted him to come back in two days.

Felipe nodded and eased down from the table. *"Dos días. Gracias."* He lifted his hand in farewell, then vanished through the door, a white bandage wrapped around his arm.

"¡Adiós!" Adam called, his thoughts tangled in the plight of the locals with their poverty and poor living conditions. His heels thudded as he crossed the tile floor and slammed the cabinet door. He needed to tell Katherine to get someone to restock all the cabinets in the examining rooms.

Adam paused, hearing his attitude. The lecture he'd heard before he came to Doctors Without Borders rose in his mind. Staff needed the ability to work and live as a team, to manage stress, to be tolerant and flexible. His shoulders drooped with the thought. Perhaps he lacked that attribute. Flexibility was for the nurses and technologists, not surgeons. But here, he had to adjust.

Instead of heading back toward the nurses' station, Adam headed for the dispensary to carry back a few supplies for the cabinet. He also had an ulterior motive. He wanted to be certain the Demerol and morphine he'd ordered had arrived, although Katherine would be irked if she knew he had checked on her.

He followed the lengthy hall to the end and turned the corner, digging into his pocket for the dispensary key, but as he neared the doorway, he saw the door was ajar.

Who would leave the room unlocked? He picked up his pace and pushed open the door.

His heart stopped. Blood froze in his veins.

"What are you doing?" he yelled.

A shot tore through him, smarting worse than a giant jejen fly.

He staggered backward. Heat and pain seared his flesh as his legs buckled.

Blackness.

Chapter Two

Pow!

Kate's heart tumbled when she heard the shot.

Pow!

Another.

Her pulse pounded as she rose on trembling legs and tore into the hallway. She hesitated, panic charging through her body. Which way? The shot had come from the left, she thought.

She rushed along the corridor, fear pumping through her limbs while glancing through doorways.

Nothing. The office was empty.

She charged forward. Turning the corner, her legs buckled, and she grabbed the wall for support. Her head spun, her ears hummed with her rising pulse.

The dispensary door gaped, and her hands shuddered as she grabbed the jamb and pulled herself around the door frame.

"Adam!"

His body lay crumpled on the floor. Blood seeped onto the tile from his head.

"Help! *¡Socorro!*" She dropped to Adam's side, feeling for a pulse. It was faint and unsteady. She pushed back his blood-soaked hair and saw a wound. Fear gripped her. Gunshot to the head? She looked again and saw no entry wound.

Kate's focus flew downward where the front of Adam's green lab coat had begun to turn a reddish brown. Blood. He'd been shot in the chest.

"*¡Dios mio! No.*" Carmen's high-pitched wail echoed in the doorway.

Kate pivoted toward the voice.

Carmen stared at Adam's body, wide-eyed, while her fingers outlined the sign of the cross on her chest. "*¿Quién hizo esto?*"

"I don't know who did this," Kate answered. She waved her hand toward the hallway. "Find Dr. Reese."

Carmen stood as if not hearing, her hands clasped near her throat as if in prayer.

"Hurry! *¡Vaya!*"

"*Sí,*" Carmen cried as she fled from the room.

"Adam," Kate intoned, hoping to rouse him. The blood oozed a darker, wider circle on his surgical jacket as Kate's fear deepened. "Adam, listen to me. Hang on."

Kate froze as another shot rang out in the distance. Her mind and body caught on a whirlwind of frenzy and fear. Who? What? Why? Questions ricocheted through her thoughts like buckshot. Dr. Reese? Dr. Valenti? Dr. Eckerd? Who was the victim this time?

Kate pulled open the lab coat, then unbuttoned his

shirt and gaped at the entry wound—the torn, burned flesh brought bile to her throat. She rose and grasped sterile pads from the shelves.

Near the doorway, she saw a carton and forced it beneath Adam's legs to elevate them. Then she pulled a blanket from a nearby shelf and covered him to ward off shock.

Kneeling, she pressed the sanitary packing against the pulsing wound. She listened to his ragged breathing as he struggled to pull air into his lungs. The shallow, raspy sound punctuated her panic.

Her fingers shifted again to his pulse, feeling the soft, erratic beat. *Lord, keep him safe.* Kate uttered the words over and over like a litany. With her other hand, Kate ran her finger along his death-white cheek, feeling the prickle of whiskers and longing to see his eyes open. Fearful, she lifted his lid and viewed only white sclera. The bright blue irises that often sent her heart spinning hid behind the socket where a sliver of color remained.

Tears pooled along her lashes, and hopelessness crushed her as she waited for Dr. Gordon Reese. Adam needed a surgeon and none were on duty tonight, and she knew Carmen would have to summon him from the nearby living quarters.

"Adam, you'll be all right. Hang on. Just lie still until we find out if anything's broken." She gazed at the handsome man lying inert beside her. He struggled for breath, and his chest shuddered with each attempt.

She checked her watch while her prayerful litany continued until the sound of running footsteps riveted her attention to the doorway.

Gordon Reese dashed into the room, his face drawn and ashen. "What's happened?" He knelt beside Kate, his trained eye studying the situation. "He needs a chest tube. The bullet punctured a lung."

Kate rose and waved Carmen from the doorway where she hovered, her hands clutched against her chest. "Get the gurney. Over here." She pointed to the metal table, in case the woman didn't understand.

Carmen nodded and eased around their crouched forms to fetch the stretcher stored along the wall.

"I heard another shot," Kate said. "Have you seen Dr. Eckerd? Dr. Valenti? Anyone?"

"No," Gordon Reese said, trying to hoist the bulk of Adam's body upward. "When we get him on the gurney, hang an IV. A thousand cc's. He'll need blood."

As she struggled to lift Adam, Dr. Valenti tore into the room. "What is this? What happened?" Blood rolled from his lip to his chin, and he looked shaken. "I struggled with them outside. Two men. One escaped, but I wrestled a gun from the other one. I shot him. I think he's dead."

"Dead?" Kate rose and beckoned Dr. Valenti to take her place. "Carmen." She motioned to the woman gawking from the hallway. "Call the police."

Carmen hurried away, and Kate prepared the IV while the doctors lifted Adam to the stretcher.

"We'll take care of this. Just hang the bag and then call Vance Memorial," Dr. Reese ordered. "We need to know if they want to airlift Adam back to Colorado Springs or somewhere else."

She nodded, spinning on her heel, and headed to the telephone. Her fingers trembled as she punched in the numbers. The time dragged as she waited for a connection to the United States, then to speak with the hospital director at Vance Memorial. She grappled to concentrate on her conversation as she described the situation. Her thoughts were on Adam and the two doctors working to save his life.

The director's order halted her thoughts when she heard his decree. "I want the team back. I want you all to come home. We'll send our staff back only after we have some answers."

"You want the team back? But what about—?"

"The other doctors can stay and run the facility. I want the Vance Memorial team here."

"Sir, I need to tell you that Dr. Valenti had a run-in with one of the burglars and shot him."

"He what? Never mind. They'll need him for questioning. Valenti can stay, but I want the rest of you to return. I'll order Medevac to airlift Adam home. You and Dr. Reese fly with him if you can."

"All right, sir," Kate said, shocked at the director's orders. "They're operating now. I'll keep you posted."

"Do that…and be careful. All of you."

She didn't have enough strength to agree or fight for the clinic's needs. When she hung up, she hurried to the operating room with his words ringing in her head.

Peeking through the small window, Kate watched Dr. Reese and Dr. Valenti hover over Adam. Fear had rankled her reasoning skills. Flying home meant she had things to do and fast.

Before she could act, Carmen appeared at her side with three men, two dressed in navy-blue short-sleeved shirts with patches on the sleeve, officers from the Santa Maria de Florès police department, and the third in plainclothes. Detective or vice squad, Kate figured.

In her minimal Spanish she explained what she knew, using Carmen as an interpreter when necessary. Their questions backlashed through her head—had she heard sounds or smelled strange odors, were doors opened or closed, were there witnesses to the shooting and who had been in the dispensary since the crime?

When she explained about Adam's surgery, the detective's glower let her know they'd contaminated the crime scene. How could she explain they couldn't stand back and let Adam die? She only shook her head and showed them the surgery taking place inside the operating room. The detective looked through the window, gave instructions to the officers, then walked away.

The younger man quizzed her again, taking down names and facts that Kate could remember while the other officer listened.

"Come," she said, guiding the young men to the dispensary. She led them along the corridor, and as they reached the doorway, the detective stepped in from the delivery entry and followed them.

She motioned the men inside, her stomach churning at the pool of blood on the floor. Not just blood, but Adam's blood. She indicated where she'd found him, his position on the floor. From that location, one officer measured distances and angles, speculating from the drugs found on the floor where the looters had stood.

The other officer donned plastic gloves and moved

about so as not to disturb evidence any more than the medical staff had destroyed earlier. While Kate watched from the hallway, the younger man pried what appeared to be two bullets from the wall beside the doorway and dropped them into plastic bags.

The detective turned his attention to a blood stain on the corner of a storage cabinet. Kate suspected it was where Adam had struck his head in the fall, the reason for the gaping wound above his temple.

They worked with speed, measuring and taking notes. When they finished, one officer closed the door and cordoned off the room.

Kate gaped at the closed door blocking their medical supplies. Somewhere in her addled mind, she thought of the people who depended on the clinic for their health-care needs. Sadness turned to anger and the emotions mingled with the fear and bewilderment that already overwhelmed her.

Outside the dispensary, the detective pointed to the delivery door. "Do you keep this locked?"

Carmen, lingering on the sidelines, translated. "Yes, always."

He opened the door and Kate followed. Outside she could see the body on the ground while officers huddled around. The detective shooed her away, but she peeked at the doorjamb anyway, wondering if it had been pried open. She saw nothing—no marks or dents. She looked closer, but the irate man ordered her away for a second time.

Kate moved inside and hurried toward the operating room. She had nothing to do now but follow orders and prepare to leave. Her breath came in gasps as she neared the surgeon. Would Adam make it back to Colorado Springs alive?

She couldn't bear to think otherwise.

Kate's body trembled with exhaustion as she willed her eyes to stay focused. She looked around the surgical waiting room at Vance Memorial Hospital, with its drab yellow walls and unimpressive framed prints. She shifted on the plastic upholstery and eyed her rumpled blouse and pants she'd worn for the past twenty hours.

The chaos of those past hours filled her mind. The surgery at the clinic, the fear, the questioning, the packing, the waiting.

She had flown back in the Medevac with Adam clinging to life with his falling blood pressure and faltering pulse. The problem had been what she feared—internal bleeding. Now she waited with Adam's parents for his second surgery.

Kate eyed her watch. Nearly two hours. She'd told his folks everything she knew about the horrible incident. The details lay muddled in her overtaxed mind, and she was glad they'd accepted her patchy description.

"Rats." Adam's father slammed his fist on the table beside his chair and sent the lamp teetering before it settled in place. "What are they doing?"

"Frank," Liza Montgomery said to her husband, her voice calm and hushed, "be patient."

"Patient! I've been more than patient. I don't understand what's keeping them." He rose, unfolding his tall, stocky frame, and paced in front of them.

Kate scrutinized the Montgomerys and wondered if

she should infringe on their privacy. Her nurse's persona took over, and she leaned forward. "Adam has internal bleeding, Mr. Montgomery. That may take time to repair...depending on where they find the problem and how extensive the damage is."

She glanced at her watch again, realizing only a minute had passed since she'd last looked. "The doctor should be in soon, I'm sure."

Frank ran his thick hand through his bushy white hair and gazed at her with vivid blue eyes canopied by shaggy white brows.

His eyes unnerved her; they were the same shade of blue as Adam's.

He gave her a subdued nod, then settled back into the chair and folded his hands in front of him while he stared at the floor.

Kate wondered if he were praying. Though he was arrogant as a peacock, Adam, she knew, was a Christian. Kate guessed his father was, too.

"So tell us about yourself, Katherine," Liza said, gazing at her with amazing green eyes and a kindly smile.

Kate froze at the suggestion. Talking about herself fell somewhere in her list of favorite activities between cleaning the toilet and scrubbing out the trash cans.

"Not much to tell," she said, hoping to dissuade the woman without being rude.

"Tell us about your work at Doctors Without Borders. Adam tells us so little."

Kate relaxed. She could talk about the clinic. "It's challenging. We deal with poverty, primitive conditions and a language barrier. We all speak a little

Spanish—very little in some cases." She gave them a halfhearted grin, the first she'd displayed in many hours. "But despite the problems, we feel blessed to provide care to people who would have none if we weren't there."

Liza shifted her rounded frame to face Kate more directly while she pushed back a graying blond curl from her rosy cheek. "I'm sure it's rewarding, and you're serving people just as our dear Lord has told us to do."

"Yes. We're making a difference," Kate agreed, filling the time by sharing stories of their living facilities, the patients they'd treated, the long hours they worked. "But it's beautiful, too," Kate said. "In spring the trumpet trees blossom with flowers. Mauve, rose, white. So lovely. The coconut palms get heavy with fruit. And the lagoon with the thick mangrove islands. And birds of every color. It glorifies the Lord's handiwork."

Liza's smile brightened. "You're a Christian."

"Yes. My mother depended on the Lord to get us through…" Kate let the words slide. "Get us through" was more than Kate meant to share about the past. Without prayer and God's presence, her childhood would have been devastated.

"Does your mother live nearby?"

Kate tried to cover her sadness. "No, she died of cancer when I was eighteen."

Liza's face skewed with sympathy. "Oh, dear, I'm so sorry."

"That was fifteen years ago. I've learned to accept it. I like to think God has a purpose for everything." Her words sounded correct, but so often Kate wished her mother had lived so today she could provide her mother with the home and security she'd never had.

"You're so right. And she must have been a wonderful mother to give you such a good upbringing…and look at you. You're a nurse. I'm sure she would be proud."

Kate gave her a nod. "Yes, she would have been. I wish she knew."

"Perhaps she does, dear. We just never know."

Frank's patience had reached its limit. He bounded from the chair and strutted across the room to the volunteer's desk. Kate watched him pointing to his watch and to the telephone. She was sure the poor woman felt intimidated. He was a powerful, impressive man, and being the mayor of Colorado Springs, he was a man who expected action. Today he wasn't getting it.

The attendant held firm, and soon Adam's father turned away, grabbed a cup of coffee from the dispenser and carried it back to the chair. "Anyone want any of this stuff? It's so strong, it could stand alone without a cup."

Kate could attest to that. The acrid smell drifted toward her and curdled her stomach. She shook her head.

Liza sent him a "No, thank you," then leaned closer to Kate. "Frank has no patience. I wish he could learn that not everyone jumps at his bidding."

Kate only smiled.

"I volunteer here, and I always feel badly for folks who have to wait so long for their loved ones," Liza said.

"You're a volunteer at Vance Memorial?"

"Yes. I'm usually at the front information desk, but I fill in where needed. Like I said, God wants us to do for others. Since I'm not a nurse or a doctor like Adam, I help in this way."

"What a lovely thing to do," Kate said. She knew many rich women would spend their time at a country club or garden club meeting…all kinds of social soirées, but here was a woman who did something for others.

"I sit on the board of the Galilee Women's Shelter, too. We do fund-raisers for the facility, help out however we can."

Kate's throat tightened, and she swallowed the emotion that strangled her. "Such a worthy cause. That must be very fulfilling."

"Indeed. It's sad to learn how many women— sometimes even children—pass through its doors."

"I can imagine," Kate said, holding back the feelings that continued to swell inside her. "I'm familiar with that center and its work. I've always admired the people who make it an option for women."

Liza's gaze searched hers, as if trying to read into her comment, sending a queasy feeling to Kate's stomach.

"Our big fund-raiser is coming up in a few months," Liza said.

Kate breathed a relieved sigh. She was grateful Liza hadn't probed about her personal life.

"Fund-raisers require much work. We always need volunteers, and it takes many hours to make it happen."

"I can imagine," Kate said, letting her ramble on while Kate nodded and smiled, but her mind was on

Adam. She knew his parents were worried, too. While his father ranted and raved, Adam's mother seemed to use chatter to ease her stress.

A surgeon finally came through the doorway, paused a moment, then headed in their direction. "Mr. and Mrs. Montgomery?"

Frank and Liza rose like soldiers snapping to attention when brass appeared. "How is he?" they asked in unison.

The surgeon's tired eyes studied their faces as if holding back something.

No. Not Adam. Kate's heart jolted as anxiety reared like an angry stallion. Kate held her breath.

Chapter Three

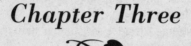

Kate's limbs quaked waiting for the surgeon to break the silence. She was concerned that Gordon Reese hadn't come to speak with the Montgomerys. He'd performed the surgery.

"Your son is in recovery, then he'll be moved to ICU. The bullet entered below the fifth intercostal space, traversed his diaphragm and punctured his stomach. We were able to stop the bleeding and make the repair."

"Why didn't they know that in Venezuela?" Frank said, his voice rising in volume.

"If he'd been conscious, Dr. Reese would have realized earlier, but the concussion masked the additional problem. If your son had been alert, he would have experienced abdominal pain. Remember, he'd already suffered a collapsed lung. Dr. Reese inserted a chest tube that saved his life."

Liza grasped Frank's arm, hearing the surgeon's

words. For Kate, the reminder was more than she wanted.

"Let's be grateful the team spotted the next problem early," the doctor said. "They notified the hospital and we were ready when they arrived."

Liza looked at the surgeon with pleading eyes. "Will he…will my son…?" Her voice quivered and she clutched her hands against her chest as if in prayer.

"He's critical…but that's to be expected. We'll know for sure in a couple of days, but for now, I'd say he's doing better than we could hope for. He was in good health before the accident, and I'm confident he'll pull through this."

Accident? Kate wanted to explain it wasn't an accident but a horrible crime. She clamped her lips and swallowed the words. Explaining wasn't her place. She was Adam's co-worker. Nothing more.

"I thought Dr. Reese performed the surgery," Kate said.

"We operated together. Gordon is exhausted. That's why I came to talk with you."

"I was on the plane with him. I know he's worn-out."

Kate was tired, too. Her thoughts soared back to the dispensary in Venezuela. She could see the blood seeping from Adam's chest. She recalled the fear and anguish she felt seeing the handsome man slumped on the floor, seemingly lifeless. She blocked the ghastly vision.

"Is he conscious now? When can we see him?" Frank asked.

"They'll let you know when you can go in," the

surgeon said, looking at Frank, then Liza. "Visiting
will be limited until he's in a regular room."

"Thank you, Doctor," Liza said. Frank grasped his
hand with a firm shake.

The surgeon stepped away. The Montgomerys
seemed to relax and settled into their seats.

Kate's heart ached but she managed to contain her
concern. Adam hadn't regained consciousness throughout the ordeal, and Kate knew what that meant. She
leaned back, hoping to conceal her worry.

"What in the good earth is an intercoastal space?"
Frank asked, looking at Kate. "It's all a bunch of
mumbo jumbo to me."

"*Intercostal* space," Kate corrected. "It's the
space between the fifth and sixth rib. The bullet went
through the chest and exited Adam's back. The damage could have been much worse. We should be very
grateful." She realized too late she'd used the word
we.

"Yes, indeed," Liza said, her gaze searching
Kate's face as if mulling over what she'd said. She
shifted her gaze toward her husband. "We should be
on our knees thanking God and not complaining,
Frank."

Before any more was said, the ICU nurse arrived
and beckoned his parents to follow.

Kate relaxed and watched them vanish through the
doorway. She longed to be with them to see for herself that Adam was all right. She knew the physical
signs and understood the monitor readings.

Her mind relived the fear she'd felt that day—the
gunshots, her confusion, the dizzy fear that weakened
her limbs, the panic she'd felt the moment she saw

Adam bleeding on the floor. At that moment, she hadn't had time to think about the why and who. She'd only had time to put pressure on the wound and do what she could to avoid shock from setting in.

But later, on the plane, she'd run the day over in her mind. Who would do this? Someone who'd been there, someone who knew where supplies were stored? Carmen? Señor Garcia? He'd been Adam's last appointment, and he had a drug problem as well as alcohol. Everyone knew that. Her thoughts had struck a dead end, just as her life had seemed to now.

Instead of brooding, she rose and stretched her arms, trying to relieve the tension that knotted down her spine. She walked to the window and looked outside. The late-afternoon sun pressed against the pane, sending its heat through the glass. Kate looked beyond the familiar parking lot to the highway.

The shock of the past few days washed over her like icy water. Her whole life had changed in a few dreadful moments in Venezuela. She'd set her course and prepared for the dramatic move to Doctors Without Borders, subleased her apartment and sold her clunker in hopes of buying a new car when she returned from her year's stint there.

So here she was now. No place to live. No car. No plans until she talked with the nursing director to see what they could do for her. Still, at the moment, all she wanted to do was see Adam, then sleep. She'd been without sleep for nearly two days. Her body trembled with fatigue and stress.

"Katherine."

Kate lifted her head and saw Mrs. Montgomery approaching her.

"I'm sure you'd like to go in for a few minutes. Please go ahead. Frank is down getting us all some fresh coffee."

Kate stood as Liza reached her. The woman grasped her fingers, her eyes dewy with tears.

"He looks a bit better," she said. "He has a little color in his cheeks. He…" Her voice faded and she covered her face with her hands.

Kate longed to wrap her arms around the gentle woman, to give her comfort, something that would ease her anxiety. But something held her back. "He'll be fine, Mrs. Montgomery. I'ye prayed incessantly since this happened."

Liza drew a shuddered breath and lifted her tear-stained face. "I'm sorry for crying. Adam's our oldest. I can't imagine—"

"It's natural to cry and worry. I've done the same, and he's just my colleague. My friend." He was her friend in a strange sense. Despite his frequent uppity attitude, they'd lived in the same compound for the past months, shared the same food, laughed at the same jokes, struggled with the same crises. If that wasn't friendship, she didn't know what was. And if Kate were truthful, her heart had taken a strange turn when it came to Adam—a turn she hated to admit.

"You go ahead, dear," Liza said, wiping her eyes with a pink lace-edged handkerchief. "I'll be fine. Frank will be here in a moment."

Kate gave the woman's arm a squeeze, her own heart skipping with anticipation, and then she headed through the doorway and down the short corridor.

She pushed the large button on the wall, and the ICU door swished open. She moved past the monitors flashing the vital signs and data and entered the room, peering into cubicles until she saw him.

Kate froze, witnessing the strong, opinionated man, now unconscious. She preferred his attitude rather than seeing him like this. His face looked pale and unexpressive. Where was the color Liza had mentioned?

"Adam." She neared his bed and stood beside his head, looking for a flicker of eyelashes or some sign of awareness.

She saw none.

"I miss your know-it-all comments, Adam. You're not going to let a little bullet in the chest keep you down, are you?"

Kate moved her fingers forward and brushed one against his cheek. She'd never touched Adam so intimately until the day he had lain sprawled on the dispensary floor when she felt the prickle of whiskers on his cheek, whiskers now more pronounced.

The image sent a chill through her, and her heart pounded with angry thumps before settling down to a steady rhythm.

"Do you hear me, Adam? Come on. Wake up and give me some of your lip." Lip. She eyed his well-formed mouth, recalling an occasional smile that lit his face…usually when he riled her. He seemed to enjoy setting her on edge.

Her gaze slid down the sheet, watching the steady rise and fall of his chest aided by a flow of oxygen. His hands lay limp at his sides, and she couldn't resist raising one and giving it a squeeze, but she resisted the desire to draw it to her lips and kiss his talented fingers—fingers that held surgical instruments and changed lives.

As she returned his hand to his side, Kate leaned closer to his ear. "Adam. Where's your spirit? Where's your irritating arrogance? Wake up and let me see those lovely blue eyes."

She pulled back, almost fearing he would open them, having heard her confession.

He didn't.

Hearing the steady sizzle of oxygen and the beeps from the equipment behind her, Kate stood a moment, gazing at the powerful man now in God's hands.

"Father, be with him," she whispered. "Give him strength and healing so he can return to his lifesaving work…and, Lord, give me direction. I'm lost right now. I don't know what will happen or where I'll go. Give me courage. In Jesus' precious name. Amen."

Her gaze swept over Adam's silent form, then feeling helpless, she turned and left the room. She pushed the button and walked into the corridor on wobbly legs.

From the waiting room doorway, she could see two others had joined the Montgomerys—a man about Adam's height with dark blond hair and a woman with blond hair cut in a short, spunky style. From a distance, she could have been a young boy dressed in jeans and a knit shirt, but her shapely figure gave her away.

Kate hesitated joining them and lingered at the threshold until Liza's voice greeted her.

"Katherine, come meet our children, and—" she

lifted a cardboard cup in the air ''—have your coffee while it's hot.''

With her urging, Kate came forward, wondering what kind of impression she would make on these two people. She knew she looked awful with no sleep and no shower.

''Katherine Darling, this is our son, Jake, Adam's younger brother, and our daughter, Colleen. She's the baby of the family.'' She smiled at Kate, then shifted her gaze to her children.

''Call me Kate,'' she said, extending her hand.

''Katherine's with Doctors Without Borders,'' Liza said. ''She's the one who found Adam after he'd been shot.''

''So you're the one,'' Jake said, taking her hand in his. ''Thank you.''

Kate saw the same blue eyes again. Looking at Colleen, she realized all of the children had their father's eyes. ''You're welcome, but please don't thank me. It's all a blur. The experience unraveled me.''

''I've never known Adam to ever be ill,'' Colleen said. ''Growing up with two older brothers, I had to learn to fend for myself. I can't picture Adam like this. Not at all.'' She ran slender fingers through her thatch of hair.

Kate could envision Colleen joining in her brother's fray. She looked as if the rough-and-tumble had rubbed off on her. Not that she wasn't attractive, but she had a spirited way about her.

''I suppose we should get it over with,'' Colleen said to her brother, giving him a playful punch in the arm. ''Standing here is making the waiting worse.''

Jake linked his arm in hers. ''Jut that chin out, sis.

You can do it, and I'll remember what you said when he's back on his feet and you want to throttle him for something.''

Colleen chuckled, they turned away and headed for ICU.

Watching the Montgomery family's support and concern sent loneliness through Kate's body. She watched Jake and Colleen pass through the doorway, arm in arm. They had the kind of relationship she'd never had, being an only child.

The kind of close relationship she might never experience in her lifetime.

Bound in blackness, Adam struggled against the weight that anchored him to the shadowy void, a smoky, spiraling existence that held him fast.

Digging his nails into the darkness, he struggled to rise. An ebony cosmos swirled to gray, then purple to red. Orange and scarlet flames licked at his body, searing a hole through his chest. The pain writhed within him, but he dragged himself forward into the inferno for Kate. She'd called to him. He'd heard her voice.

Danger surrounded her as the blaze surged at her feet. His own scorched flesh reeked as he neared her. He called her name, but his parched throat and dried mouth turned his words to dust.

The fire became a whirlwind, like a dervish—yellow, coral and crimson—fading, vanishing into the abyss, taking Kate with it.

His charred body made a final grasp at nothing but darkness.

* * *

Kate watched the ICU door swing open as Adam's brother and sister vanished inside.

Dizziness caught her off guard. She grabbed the arm of a chair to steady herself.

"Are you all right?" Liza asked, shifting to Kate's side. "You're exhausted, I'm sure." She patted the seat cushion. "Sit now and drink some of this coffee. Have you eaten?"

Eaten? Kate hadn't eaten for hours. Food hadn't crossed her mind.

"I'm just tired."

"You should go home, dear. You need food and rest. Do you live in town?"

Her question dropped like a weight on Kate's shoulders. "I did before I went to Venezuela. I sublet my apartment."

"Sublet your apartment? Oh, dear." She turned to her husband. "Did you hear that, Frank? The poor girl sublet her apartment."

Kate tried to smile. "I thought it was a good idea at the time. I'd volunteered for a year, and I was being frugal. I even sold my car. It was a junker, and I figured…" She shrugged. "Now I don't know what will happen. I'm not sure if I'll be sent back or…"

Or what? Her future was hanging by a thread.

Kate realized she was foolish to sit there and wonder. She needed to act. "I'll have to get a room somewhere until I know what's happening."

"Nonsense," Liza said. "We'll think of something." She turned to her husband. "Won't we, Frank?"

Adam's father straightened. "Certainly. You saved our son's life." He glanced at his wife as if to make sure he was heading in the right direction. She gave him a subtle nod and smiled.

"The least we can do," he continued, "is invite you to stay with us until you make other arrangements. We have plenty of room."

"Too much room for the two of us," Liza added. Then she wagged her finger at Kate. "And no disagreement now. You'll go home with us."

"Well, I…"

Kate's voice faded when she saw Dr. Reese appear in the doorway. The Montgomerys rose, and Liza clutched her husband's arm as if expecting the worst.

Gordon Reese shook his head. "He's fine, stable, and I don't expect a change until morning. I'd suggest you go home and get some rest. Sitting here won't help Adam. If there's a change, we'll call you immediately, but I'm certain he's going to be fine." He gave Kate a nod.

Liza looked at her husband, her eyes seeming to question if they should listen to the doctor's suggestion.

"You'll call us?" Frank asked. "No funny business."

Gordon Reese chuckled. "No funny business. We'll call if there's any change…good or bad."

"Thank you. We'd appreciate that."

"I told your son and daughter the same thing. They're staying for a few minutes longer. They said they'll see you back at your house."

Frank extended his hand. "Thank you, Doctor."

"You're welcome. Now get some rest. You, too, Kate," he said, looking at her. "You're all welcome to come back tomorrow morning whenever you're ready.''

''Tomorrow morning,'' Liza repeated. ''Yes. That will be fine. Thank you.''

Gordon Reese backed away, and Kate watched him head through the door, feeling better having heard his prognosis.

The Montgomerys gathered up their belongings and ushered Kate out of the waiting room. Discomfort slowed her footsteps, discomfort and exhaustion. She had no business staying with the Montgomerys, but tonight she had no other options, especially when her mind felt knotted in a tight jumble like thread that had tangled and had been rewound on the spool, knots and all.

Outdoors, the early-evening air covered her with dry heat. She slid into the back seat of their sleek, black car and clung to the door handle to stay erect. If she leaned back, she knew she would fall asleep.

The downtown scene flashed past, familiar yet blurred by her weary eyes and her wavering thoughts. They passed the Broadmoor Hotel and sprawling homes that only peeked from behind lush landscaping. With Adam's father being the mayor, Kate assumed they would live in a nice part of town, but this was more than she'd expected. She'd never seen the Colorado Springs mayor's residence. She had no idea where it was located.

When the car slowed and turned, Kate willed her eyelids open and focused on the wide drive leading to an expanse of freshly cut lawn. Ahead sat a massive redbrick home with beige trim and brown shutters at the wide French pane windows.

How often had Adam visited this house? she wondered. What she did know was the family who lived here was far out of her league, just as Adam was. She'd admired Adam from afar—his talent, his generosity, his handsome frame, his sparkling blue eyes.

Afar was about as close as she would ever get.

Chapter Four

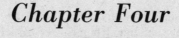

Standing in the Montgomery living room, Kate marveled at the coziness of the huge house. Someone's efforts had brightened what might have been a dark, ponderous room by understating the wide woodwork and dark paneled inserts with colorful walls and chintz upholstery. Antiques mingled with traditional furniture were placed in conversational groupings. The room looked genial.

Kate took in the artwork, the abundance of antique dishes adorning the mantle and corner cabinet, and the colorful toss pillows, remembering her meager childhood, her less-than-cozy dwelling.

"Set your luggage in the hall, Katherine. I'll have Jake carry it up for you when he arrives."

Kate stepped into the foyer and dropped her luggage beside the stairs. She gazed upward at the rounding staircase that led to rooms she speculated would be as tasteful as the one she'd seen.

"Make yourself at home," Liza said behind her.

Kate spun around. "The house is lovely. Are the mayors' families allowed to change the decor? This really looks like you. Such delicate touches."

Liza chuckled. "The official mayor's residence is closer to the city offices. When Frank was elected, he chose to stay in our own home, and I was pleased. We raised all three children here. This is where our hearts are."

Kate's muddied mind sorted out her words. This was Adam's childhood home. Her earlier comment brought embarrassment. "I didn't know. I thought I could see your handiwork. It's very comfortable."

"Thank you. I do want our friends to feel welcome here…and please consider yourself a friend, Katherine."

"Then call me Kate. My friends do." *Except Adam*, she mused.

"Kate it is. Now, as I said, you go and make yourself comfortable. I know we're all hungry, and I'll just go and see what I can rummage up."

"Please, let me help," Kate said.

"Are you sure? I know you've been through so much."

Kate shook her head. "It'll help me keep the awful memories off my mind." *And keep me awake,* she thought.

"Then come along." Liza motioned for her to follow.

Her gaze lingered on the wide staircase for a moment; she imagined Adam as a child sliding down the banister or taking the steps two at a time the way boys do. She dragged her thoughts to the present and made her way behind Adam's mother to the kitchen.

Kate gaped as she stood inside the large room with a center island where pots and pans hung, their copper bottoms gleaming just as she'd seen in magazines. She never thought people really used them.

To her surprise, Liza pulled one down and set it on the stove. "Our housekeeper does much of the cooking, but today's she's off so I take over. It's nothing to prepare a meal for only us, but today, my guess is Jake and Colleen will join us."

"What can I do?" Kate asked.

Liza rubbed her cheek and stared into the refrigerator. "Hmm. Something fast is what we need."

Kate watched as Adam's mother pulled out a large ham, a crockery pot full of baked beans and fresh salad greens from the refrigerator. "You'll find some red skins in the little pantry, there." She pointed to the door on the left. Kate found the potatoes, and she and Liza worked side by side, preparing the meal.

Soon voices echoed from the hallway, and Colleen made her entrance into the kitchen. She sneaked a sliver of ham from the stack and curled it into her mouth. "Can I help?" she asked between chews.

"You can set the table," Liza said.

Somewhere in the haze of exhaustion, Kate found herself seated between Liza and Colleen at the dining room table. The fine china and sterling seemed a paradox to the simple home-cooked meal, but Kate accepted the family's refined ways and placed the linen napkin on her rumpled pants.

Frank stretched his arms toward his wife and son, a seeming family tradition, and Kate grasped the two hands extended to her. They bowed their heads, hands joined, making a circle around the table, while

Adam's father offered the blessing and asked the Lord for Adam's safekeeping.

Even though the meal consisted of leftovers, the food was delicious, but Kate could only nibble at her meal. Despite being hungry, she felt too tired to swallow. The family conversation rolled as naturally as if she weren't a stranger. While Adam's father seemed blustery, she saw a gentleness when it came to his children, like a growling canine who, getting close enough, licks the intruder's hand.

Kate had little to offer with her mind and body weary and her self-esteem sinking fast as she sat at the gleaming wood table and chairs, cherry or fruitwood with Queen Anne legs and tapestry seat cushions. The large china cabinet glinted with sparkling cut glass and colorful antique dishes.

Kate listened to the conversation. At first the talk dwelled on the family's concern for Adam. Colleen and Jake asked questions about Doctors Without Borders and their lives in Venezuela. Kate tried to answer, though her tongue and teeth were no longer in sync.

But soon the conversation drifted to more personal topics. Adam's home. Adam's family. Adam's life. She clung to every thread of his amazing world.

Frank speared a dollop of butter with his knife and spread it across a thick piece of bread. "I talked to your uncle Joe yesterday." He forked a slab of ham and lay it on top.

"How is he?" Jake asked.

Liza eyed the bread and meat. "Frank, you're not making a sandwich at dinner, are you?" Her gaze slid to Kate's while her cheeks flushed. "We have a guest."

"I certainly am," he said, taking a chomp out of the concoction. "And Kate can make her own sandwich if she wants."

Liza shook her head and gave Kate a shrug. Kate grinned and slid a piece of potato into her mouth.

"So what's up with Uncle Joe?" Jake asked.

"Mad as a hornet."

"What happened?"

"Barclay again." Frank dropped his sandwich onto the plate and slapped his hand on the tabletop. "The man's stealing business right out from under him… and it's not the first time."

"You mean Montgomery Construction lost another bid?" Jake said.

Frank nodded. "It's the fourth, and this time Joe said they gave a low bid. He told me he knew no one could underbid him. The company would have barely made a profit." He rapped his knuckles on the table beside his plate. "I'd like to get my hands around that crook's neck."

"Dad," Colleen said, "you don't know he's a crook. He's a businessman. A mogul."

"Mongrel is right," Frank said.

Colleen didn't give up. "Dad. Look at those gorgeous hotels he owns all over town. The guy must know what he's doing. You can't blame him because he doesn't give his business to Montgomery Construction."

"You don't know what you're talking about, Colleen." Her father shook his fork at her. "I co-owned Montgomery Construction once. Remember that. I know about business. That guy's doing something shady.''

''Frank,'' Liza said, ''let's enjoy our dinner.''

''Who won the bid?'' Jake asked, ignoring his mother's plea for a relaxing meal.

''Same company as last time. Elroy Construction.''

Jake shook his head. ''Never heard of it.''

''Ready for coffee and pie?'' Liza rose and gathered the empty plates around her.

Kate covered a grin, watching her hostess's ploy to distract them from their conversation.

''What kind of pie, Mom?'' Colleen asked.

''Aunt Fiona's apple pie. We picked up two a couple days ago.''

''Aunt Fiona's?'' Jake asked. ''My favorite.''

Liza smiled. ''How about à la mode? Vanilla ice cream?''

''I'll take a big piece,'' Jake said.

Kate decided to pass on dessert. If she didn't skip the pie, she'd pass out at the table for sure. Sleep was the only thing that sounded good to her.

Rest didn't come easy for Kate. Her body jerked and her eyes flew open as she began to sink into sleep. She'd been up two full days, and her senses had set themselves on the edge of awareness.

Kate couldn't believe they'd given her the use of Adam's old bedroom. Her eyes took in every nook and cranny as she imagined Adam as a child. Colleen had mentioned he'd been a science buff even then, intent on his microscope, pricking his own finger for blood, analyzing insects he'd dragged in from outside.

Before she'd lain down, Kate had stood at the wide

window, gazing out at the sprawling yard. A huge maple stood outside the pane, its branches almost touching the glass. She'd wondered if Adam ever used the limbs to sneak out at night when he was a teen. She'd grinned at her silly imagination. She'd seen too many movies.

With relentless curiosity, her thoughts clung to Adam. Not the Adam she'd seen unconscious at Vance Memorial, but the Adam she imagined as a youth and the grown-up Adam she knew in Venezuela.

Even with his moments of impudence, he had made her laugh and entertained her with his interest in nature. She remembered one evening when the clinic's interior had become stifling, and she and Adam had run into each other outdoors, trying to catch a breath of fresh air. They'd found a gentle breeze and stood together admiring the late-afternoon sky. Appreciating the blessing, each had responded to the beauty of the sunset, its colors spreading across the horizon like pastel silk unraveling on a misty blue lake.

She recalled other days they had both marveled at the birds. Colorful parrots and tropical creatures she'd never seen before except perhaps at a zoo—large banana-curved beaks and plumage the spectrum of primary colors. Their chatter filled the daytime, reverberating with unique whistles and plaintive calls that punctuated the solitude of the compound.

One day Adam had joined her and two other staff members on a free afternoon to visit the lagoon. They saw the mangroves with their long roots extending into the water like legs on a spider. Adam had been curious that day and had studied them so closely that when an animal had skittered in the bushes, the noise had sent him flying backward. They had all laughed, and she'd felt pleased seeing Adam laugh at himself.

Kate covered her head with a pillow, then counted backward from a hundred. Finally, somewhere between three and three-thirty, she drifted off, but before the sun rose, she awakened with no hope of falling back to sleep.

Concern provoked her thoughts. She rose, took a quick shower, dressed and called a taxi. Downstairs, she found a tea bag and popped a mug of water into the microwave, figuring she would buy her much-needed coffee at the hospital.

By the time she swallowed the last of the black pekoe, the taxi's headlights flashed across the windows. She hurried outside before he honked and slumped in the back of the cab, wishing she could catch a few minutes' rest.

Solace finally came when Kate stood beside Adam's bed in ICU. She spent the hours ambling back and forth between the waiting room and his bedside.

"Adam," she whispered. "Use that attitude of yours, that self-importance I've seen so often, and wake up. Fight. Don't let this get you."

His finger was connected to a pulse oximeter. Kate touched his hand, rubbing her palm over his cool skin. "Adam. Let's pray together."

She leaned closer to his ear and murmured the prayer she'd said so often, asking God to renew his strength and spirit, to make him whole again.

When she'd said the Amen, she lifted her hand and

touched his face. "Adam, wake up. You must make it through this. You're loved by so many people."

She turned away, realizing that, without question, she was becoming one of them.

Kate lifted her gaze when she heard footsteps and saw Adam's parents step into the hospital waiting room.

When Liza saw her, she hurried to Kate's side. "How's Adam?"

"They did an EEG this morning. He seems to be doing a little better."

"He's conscious?" Liza's eyes brightened with her words.

"No. But his vital signs are good."

Mrs. Montgomery's face sagged with disappointment.

"His breathing has improved," Kate added, hoping to cheer her. "I'm guessing they'll take the chest tube out soon."

"That would be wonderful," Liza said. "What were the results of his EEG?"

"Adam's not back yet. I expect we'll hear something soon. The doctor usually stops by once he's read the test results."

Liza dropped her bag on an empty seat and wrung her hands. "This waiting is so stressful."

"It is." Kate massaged the tension in her neck, then scooted deeper into the cushion, leaned her head back and closed her eyes. She'd fought sleep all night, and now it seemed to overtake her.

"I wonder if he's back and they…"

Kate pulled herself upward and opened her eyes.

Liza regarded her face. "I'm sorry, dear. You look so tired, and I disturbed you. I apologize."

"No need. I was just resting my eyes."

"I feel so badly you couldn't sleep last night. Was the bed uncomfortable? I know it's difficult to sleep when—"

"It wasn't the bed. That felt wonderful. I was just too wound up. I'll sleep better tonight."

"I hope so," Liza said, sinking in the chair beside Kate. "It's so kind of you to stay here day in and day out like this…for Adam."

Her words charged up Kate's back. "We were close in Venezuela…working together constantly. I can't help but be concerned."

"I understand," Liza said. "You're a kindhearted young woman."

"Thank you," Kate said, not knowing how to respond since her motivation was selfish.

Kate's gaze drifted toward the door, and a doctor stepped into the room. He gave her a nod and headed their way.

"Mr. and Mrs. Montgomery?"

Kate struggled to keep from rising. Liza stood and joined her husband.

"Yes," Frank said.

"The EEG shows no permanent damage. We'll continue with analgesics for pain and keep an eye on him. I noted some extensive swelling, but hopefully that will subside and he'll regain consciousness soon."

"Is there anything we can do to help?" Liza asked.

"Brain stimulation. Talk to him. Patients can often hear. They just can't respond."

Liza nodded. "I'll feel better once I see him this morning."

"He should be back in his room now if you'd like to check. Once they remove the chest tube, he'll be going up to the surgical floor later today."

"That's great news," Frank said.

The physician agreed, then departed.

Liza turned to Kate. "We'll go in for a few minutes."

"You go ahead."

His mother clasped her bag, then took her husband's arm and headed toward the exit.

Kate watched them leave. She'd tried to keep her attitude hopeful, but she wasn't as optimistic as the physician. Adam had been unconscious too long.

She'd worked with concussion patients before, but Adam's injury seemed worse. The corner of the cabinet impacted his head above the temple. Wounds like that could cause diffuse axonal injury that resulted in disrupting the neural connections. Time could regenerate the damage, but Adam could be left with significant impairment. The possibility crushed Kate's hopes.

Pushing herself from the chair, she rose and left the waiting room. She took the elevator to the second floor where she found the chapel empty. She stood at the back, struck by the dramatic stained-glass window at the front. Brightened by sunlight, its colors spread out along the beige carpet, leaving it dappled with red, blue, purple and green.

Kate sank into the last pew and closed her eyes. She needed God's help—safety for Adam and guidance for her own upside-down world. Wrapped in a moment of silence, she spoke to God, the way she'd done since childhood. Somehow the Lord came through whenever she needed Him the most.

Her prayer centered around Adam, asking God to heal him and return him to good health, unaffected by the horrible wounds he'd received. She prayed for the Lord's loving guidance to provide her life a new direction. Though she longed to return to Venezuela, she knew God was in charge. Perhaps He had something different in mind to give her life purpose. She would accept the Lord's will as she'd always done.

Opening her eyes, Kate was gripped by the vivid window in front of her—not the colors, but the scene of Jesus healing the sick. His hands lay on the eyes of a blind man who knelt before him. Nearby, another man stood with his weight supported by crutches. The look on the men's faces awed Kate, seeing the hope and trust of those who were ill who waited for healing.

Kate carried the thought into her life. Did she have that kind of hope and trust? Today she worried about her future and what she would do about a place to stay until things were sorted out. She stopped herself in midthought. The Lord had sustained her through a difficult childhood. She felt confident God would not let her down.

Feeling uplifted by the depiction on the stained glass and by her prayer, Kate rose and stepped into the corridor. She needed to speak to the nursing director. She didn't want to put it off any longer. Her destiny lay on the outcome of her superior's decisions.

Kate's footsteps tapped along the tile floor as she returned to the elevator and traveled upward to the administration floor. Hopefully today, she'd know her immediate plans, anyway.

Chapter Five

When Kate returned to the waiting room, Liza and Frank weren't there, but Frank's jacket and newspaper still lay on the chair, and Kate assumed the couple was with Adam. She sank into the seat, grabbed a magazine and flipped through the pages, but her mind was miles away, pleased she'd at least resolved what the hospital had planned for her. She leaned her head against the back of the seat and closed her eyes. Weariness had overcome her again, but her rest was short.

"His coloring looks better," Liza said, triggering Kate to open her eyes.

"I thought so, too," Kate said.

"They sent us out because they're going to remove the chest tube now." Liza moved her tote bag and sank beside Kate.

"That's wonderful news." Kate felt her heart lurch. "Then he'll go up to the surgical floor. That's so much better."

"It will be." Liza rested her elbow on the arm of

the chair and leaned her cheek against her fist. "I'm having a terrible time seeing Adam this way. He's always been so intense, so in charge. Now he's so quiet and—"

"He'll be himself once he wakes," Frank said, settling in the seat beside his wife. He rested the *Colorado Springs Sentinel* in his lap.

Liza opened her fist and massaged her cheek with her palm. "I remember when Adam was a little boy he always had his nose in a book or his eye over a microscope. When they were children, Jake and Colleen always complained about Adam while they played hide-and-seek. He would vanish into the thicket and, instead of playing the game, would study the striations in tree bark or analyze the insects. He's always been like that. So aware of everything."

Kate understood what Liza meant. Adam was intense. He didn't let a thing pass that he didn't analyze or demand a solid answer for. "I'm sure seeing him this way has been difficult."

Frank kneaded the back of his neck. "You know, I'm proud of my son and I've always tried to respect what he wanted to do with his life, especially if he was serving others, but…Venezuela. I wasn't happy about that."

Liza shifted and rested her hand on Frank's arm. "We always support our children, but Frank and I were concerned about Adam's decision. I wish he could be more like other men his age—happily married with a family. We've encouraged him to date. Jake and Colleen are as bad about settling down. I just wish—"

"Liza, stop your perpetual matchmaking," Frank

said, lifting the newspaper and using it as a pointer. "Our children are adults and can find their own mates and make their own decisions without your help." He gave Kate a frustrated look and shook his head.

Liza's shoulders drew up with her decisive rebuttal. "Maybe they can find their own mates, Frank, but they haven't yet. None of them. I'd like grandchildren before I'm in my grave."

Frank lowered the newspaper and coiled it into a cylinder. "You'll be sending us all to our graves with your incessant prattle about it."

Her shoulders drooped as if his comment had let the air out of her.

Kate began to think she should leave and let them argue privately. She guessed the disagreement was an old one. The Montgomerys quieted and Kate's thoughts returned to Adam. Would he be back from the procedure yet? "I was thinking that—"

"Look at this. It makes me sick." Frank interrupted, poking at the first page of the newspaper. "Big fight at the Longhorn Saloon. Drinking. Drugs. They arrested sixteen."

Liza gave Kate an apologetic look. "Frank, Kate was talking."

Frank lowered the paper and opened his mouth as if to apologize.

"No, please," Kate said, flagging her hand. "Problems like that are stressful."

Liza settled back while Frank continued. "We've had more drug arrests over the past few months. I see seedy gangs hanging around the streets…but they're not doing anything illegal. The cops can't arrest them for standing there."

"The city needs better loitering laws," Liza said.

Frank gave a harumph. "You try to stop them from loitering, you get freedom of assembly complaints."

"I think we should let the police department handle it, dear." Liza crossed her legs and shifted her focus to Kate. "Did you speak to the nursing director yet?"

Kate noticed Liza's ploy to change the subject. It worked, and Frank returned to his reading.

Kate straightened her back. "The director suggested I take a week to rest with pay and pull myself together after the incident."

"That was a very considerate offer," Liza said.

"Yes, it was. Looks like a week from next Monday my life should get back to normal. I'll go back on my regular shift."

"Which is that?" Liza gave her a questioning look.

"I work the late shift on the surgical floor," Kate said.

"The late shift." Liza's face brightened. "I imagine you feel better knowing things are settled."

"Settled for now," Kate said. "They'd like me to go back to Venezuela—if I'm willing—once the situation's been resolved. I'll have to make that decision one day, but for now, I'm trying to stop my head from reeling." Kate gave Adam's mother a halfhearted smile. "The only decision I must make now is finding a place to stay."

Liza lowered her head a moment, then turned to her husband. "Frank."

His mind must have been preoccupied because he jumped to attention. "What is it?"

"What do you think if we give Kate the extra key to Adam's town house?"

"Adam's place?" His bushy eyebrows lowered into a frown.

Liza pressed her hands together. "It's just sitting there, and I doubt if Adam will need it for another week or so. What do you think, Frank?"

His brows lifted as he shrugged one shoulder. "I see no problem. Tonight we'll find the key."

"There, dear, you can stay in Adam's town house. It's very nice. Then you can find something more permanent at your leisure."

"Thank you so much…if it won't be an inconvenience."

"How could it be?" Liza gave Kate's arm a pat.

Their generosity overwhelmed her, and Kate covered a grin at the matter-of-fact way they'd solved her problem.

Frank rose and stretched. "They suggested we go home for a while and come back later. What do you say?"

"I think we could all use some rest," Liza said. "Especially you, Kate. Would you like to go back with us and try to rest awhile?"

Kate didn't want to leave, but her weary body and blurry eyes helped her face facts. "I think I'll go in to see Adam a minute if you don't mind, and then I will go back with you for a while."

"That's fine, dear. Take your time."

Kate rose and hurried from the room. She said a silent thank-you for Adam's parents who'd opened their hearts and their door to her. God always had a way of resolving issues before she had time to worry about them.

*   *   *

Following a good night's sleep, Kate returned to the hospital. This time she brought a paperback, but her mind fluttered over the words like leaves from a tree, her thoughts spiraling and tossing on an uneasy breeze. Though fear still weighted her hope, she felt better seeing Adam out of the ICU and on the surgical floor—her wing when she returned to work.

Time dragged, but she'd been miserable sitting alone at the Montgomerys' while her thoughts had been here, in his room.

Voices drifted in from the corridor, and Kate looked toward the doorway. Expecting to see a nurse, she was surprised when Colleen sailed in.

"Hi," Colleen said, a welcoming smile lighting her face.

"He's about the same," Kate said, hoping her comment sounded casual. Colleen's expression asked questions. Why was Kate here so often? What was going on between her and Adam? She felt the queries without hearing the words.

"I'd hoped he might be awake," Colleen said, dropping a tote bag on the floor and leaning over the bed. "Hey, you. Wake up."

She ran her slender fingers through her scruffy mane and sank into the chair by the bed. "Adam. It's Colleen. Open your eyes." She waited, then glanced at Kate and gave her a disappointed look.

"It's discouraging," Kate said, feeling very disheartened herself.

Silence hung in the air and Kate searched for something to talk about. "Your mom mentioned you work for the *Colorado Springs Sentinel*. Sounds like an interesting job.''

Colleen swiveled in her chair to face Kate. ''It can be. In fact, this next story—if my editor approves—might really be interesting.''

''What's that?''

''Sam Vance—have you met him?''

''No. Who is he?''

''He's a detective and one of Adam's old friends. Anyway, he called and suggested a story idea…and I like it. A feature on women affected by spouses involved in misdemeanors—fights, drugs and especially domestic violence. Sam thought it would help raise awareness on the rising crime rate and its effect on families in the city. I think it's a great idea. Don't you?''

''Sure,'' Kate said. ''Any time you make the community aware of a problem it helps everyone.''

''That's what I thought,'' Colleen said. She gestured to her tote bag. ''I have a list of the men arrested last night in the fight at the Longhorn Saloon and men involved in domestic violence in the past months. I'm thinking women will talk to a reporter faster than they will the police.''

''I think you're right,'' Kate said.

Colleen's eyes twinkled. ''Hopefully, I'll get what Sam wants and a good story on top of it. I'll need statistics, too. I might get something from the Galilee Women's Shelter although they're pretty close-mouthed.''

''They have to be to protect the families there.''

Colleen gave a toss of her head. ''I know, but my mother works with Jessica Mathers. She's the development director of the shelter. She works on fund-raisers and project development. That might give me an in.''

She glanced at her watch and rose. ''I suppose I'd better get back to the paper.'' She leaned over her brother again and called his name, but Adam didn't budge.

''Disappointing,'' Colleen said, then shrugged. ''Hopefully next time. He has to wake up sometime. I have to tell him I love him…just in case he doesn't know.'' She dipped down, kissed Adam's cheek and grabbed her tote. ''See you soon. By the way, Dad found the keys. I'll help you move to Adam's when I can grab a minute.''

''Great,'' Kate said, watching her hustle from the room. ''Thanks.''

Everyone needed Adam to wake for their own reasons—Colleen, to say ''I love you,'' and Kate…to only think it.

The police were anxious, too. Kate's back stiffened at the memory of the police hovering over Adam while he struggled for life. She'd seen it in movies—cops interrogating a dying man—but this wasn't make-believe. This was real, and Adam deserved better.

The late-afternoon sun streamed through the window, warming her back and taking away the chill that had settled over her when she'd begun to feel so cynical. Why did she insist on thinking the worst? So often she asked the Lord for help and then focused on the worst scenario possible.

Lord, keep me uplifted, she thought as she fingered the novel's pages while her focus settled on Adam's face.

Startled, she caught her breath.

His eyelashes flickered once.

Again.

Had it been real?

She rose and leaned above him. ''Adam. Wake up.'' She waited a moment, then shook his arm. ''Adam.''

Nothing. No response.

Had it been only her imagination?

Disappointed, she returned to her chair. An unexpected chill rippled down her arms, even though the sun licked at the windows.

A sound.

She stopped breathing.

A groan.

She rose again and tiptoed across the room, afraid she'd been wrong while praying she'd been right.

Silence again.

Adam wrestled in the darkness. The dank pit held the stench of cold, sulphured ash. For a moment he saw light above him, a ray of hope, but the brightness faded and fear covered him like a mucky river, dragging him into its acrid depths. Fear captured his breath while he smothered in a wave of horror.

He sensed it. Kate. She needed him. He heard her calling his name over and over. He'd struggled to rise from the abyss. His arms flailed and his broken nails dug into the crumbling earth.

Something malevolent surrounded him. His muscles knotted with anguish seeing Kate ahead of him in the murky haze, pursued by the evil one. He stretched his hand forward, but she soared from his grasp, flying closer to the black shrouded one.

Again a soft glow beckoned. A flicker of starlight in a midnight sky. He grasped his courage, pulling his weight upward.

"Adam."

He heard Kate's voice, pleading him to climb toward the soft glow. His hand lay against something soft and cool. He tried to brush his fingers along the surface, but he seemed bound in place with wire.

His eyes flickered. A hum reached his ears. Sounds and odors, familiar yet strange. His eyelids felt weighted, but he willed them to open.

The glare blinded him. A square of brilliant light framing an angel. Heaven. He'd struggled through hell and found heaven. Adam tried to speak to the angel, but she remained still, her head bent, a golden halo circling her like spun gold.

He opened his mouth to speak and heard only a groan.

The angel moved. She rose and floated toward him, her hand outstretched.

Death. It beckoned so sweetly.

Chapter Six

"Adam." A voice penetrated the haze.

Through half-closed eyes, he saw her tears.

"Adam. Wake up."

Her cool fingers touched his cheek and sent fire down his limbs as awareness settled in.

"Katherine?"

"Praise God, you're awake."

Her soft voice wrapped around him like silk. "Where am I? What happened?"

"You've been unconscious."

As she spoke, he saw her push the nurse's call button.

"Do you remember what happened?" she asked.

Confusion riddled his memory. Adam shook his head, then grimaced. He grabbed the pain that burned in his chest.

"Be careful. You've had a chest tube removed."

A nurse's voice hummed through the speaker. "Can I help you?"

"Adam Montgomery is conscious. Would you notify a doctor? And please call his parents."

As the static clicked off, Kate sat beside him.

He felt his eyes close again. Sounds floated around him like distant waves and sleep seemed his friend.

"Adam. Wake up." He felt her hand against his arm.

He forced open his eyes and squinted at her through heavy lids. Weight pressed against his chest, and a dull ache throbbed near his abdomen. He lowered his hand and felt bandages.

"Are you in pain?" Kate asked.

His parched mouth restricted the words that rattled in his head. Instead he gave her a nod.

In his peripheral vision Adam watched her pour water from the carafe into a paper cup and unwrap a straw. "Take a small sip."

When he pulled forward, the pain worsened, and he clamped his jaw to hold back a moan. Why was Kate hovering over him? What had happened? He let the cool water wash over his sawdust tongue and moisten his cracked lips.

Kate pulled away the straw. "Don't drink too much. You'll be sick."

Be sick? Right now he felt as if he'd been thrown from a wild horse. He let his gaze drift on the pale beige walls and white ceiling. "Where am I?"

"Vance Memorial. You're home."

Home? The words startled him, sending his heart bucking on the wild horse that he was sure had thrown him. "What happened?"

"Don't you remember?" A look of concern shot across her face. "You were shot by thieves."

"Shot?" He lowered his hand to his stomach again, then winced at the pressure and removed his hand. Was she playing games with him. "Thieves? I don't know what you're talking about." He heard his voice heighten, and he tried to sit up, but pain overwhelmed him and he fell back on the bed.

"Try not to get riled, Adam. The doctor should be here soon."

"Don't tell me what to do," he said, more determined than ever to sit up. He tried again, but weakness overcame him and he crumpled back against the sheet.

"It's for your own good. If you injure yourself, you'll be back in ICU."

ICU? Her words felt like a slap across his cheek. He looked at the wall clock. Frustration filled him. It had to be daytime because he saw light through the window. But what day? Fear and anger exploded in his head. "Leave me alone. Mind your own business."

Kate's eyes widened, and color drained from her face. She rose and returned to the chair by the window as if keeping her distance from him.

Good riddance, he thought.

But seeing her there triggered his waking memories. He remembered the glowing light and the form in white with a halo. He'd presumed she was an angel. Kate, an angel? If he weren't in such pain, he'd have laughed at the thought.

Now, she sat there again with the window at her back. His gaze lingered on the sunlight glinting through her blond tresses, like an aura of gold...like a halo. Her pale skin and white blouse added to the illusion.

Katherine. Kate. Something tugged at his memory. Kate in jeopardy. His dreams rolled back like mucky water from a drain. Horrible and raw. The blackness. The stench. The fire. The searing pain. The helpless feeling that Kate was in danger and he couldn't save her. He widened his eyes, praying the thoughts would leave him.

Shifting to his side, Adam let the pain roll through his chest until he'd settled himself. He watched Kate across the room, sitting in silence and staring toward the doorway. He'd hurt her feelings. How long had she been here? How long had he been here?

"What day is this?" he asked.

"Friday."

"Friday?"

"July ninth."

The date fell into his mind like a chunk of concrete. July ninth. The last he remembered was July sixth. He'd treated Señor Garcia. He had no recollection beyond that moment. In his peripheral vision, Adam spotted movement at the doorway.

"Welcome back to the living."

Adam focused on a white lab coat and a familiar face. "Hey, Doc."

Robert Fletcher moved to his side. "This is a sneaky way to get a vacation."

"Trust me." Adam winced again as he shifted back against the sheets. "It's no vacation."

"Pain?"

Adam shrugged, but he knew he couldn't fool Fletcher.

"We've had you on a drip, but now that you're awake we can wean you off that. I'd prefer you take Vicidon by mouth."

"You're the doctor," Adam said, trying to stay lighthearted in the midst of his aching confusion.

"Reese will be in to see you. He was your surgeon so he can give you the details."

Surgery? His fingers shifted over the wide bandage. What surgery? And when? He clamped his teeth to avoid spitting out his frustration. "Thanks."

Fletcher jotted notes on the chart and stepped back. "I'll check on you later."

Adam only nodded and watched him leave.

Kate remained silent, and Adam's heart softened. If today was July ninth, he'd been out of it for three days. Had she been here the whole time? Had she been in peril, too…like his dreams suggested? "Are you all right?"

She turned her head toward him. "Me? I'm fine."

"How long have you been here?"

"Today? About ten or eleven hours."

Her words wove through his thoughts in knots. Ten or eleven hours? Why? Why did she stay so long? The answer came as quickly as the question. Because she was Kate. No matter what, she cared about people. He'd seen it so many times in Venezuela. She was an angel of mercy.

Remembering his dreams, the thought made him feel foolish. "I thought you were an angel."

Her head jolted upward. "You what?"

"Thought you were an angel." He lifted his arm to gesture, but discomfort shot through him.

"Be careful," she said, rising. "You were hurt

badly, Adam. It'll be a while before you feel like yourself.''

That might be for the better, he thought, remembering how he'd annoyed her so often with his comments. ''When I opened my eyes you were sitting in the chair with the sunlight in your hair and dressed in white. I saw the halo around your head…and thought I'd left hell and made it to heaven.''

Kate's face twisted to a wry smile. ''Then you knew it was a dream. When you leave this world, I doubt if Satan will let go of you.''

Touché. ''I deserved that,'' he said, realizing the light was giving him a headache.

''No, you don't.''

Her eyes searched his and he felt drawn to smooth the stress from her cheeks. ''Tell me what happened that day.''

''The day you were shot?''

He nodded.

''You don't remember?''

He shook his head, then fingered his temple to quell the pounding.

''Headache?'' Kate asked.

''A little one. The light hurts my eyes.''

She rose and pulled the curtain as she spoke. ''You must have gone to the dispensary for some reason. Do you remember that?''

He pushed his mind back in time. He remembered Garcia, and when he left, yes…Adam recalled heading to the dispensary. ''The examining room was short of meds. I think I was going down to—''

Adam faltered, remembering he'd planned to check

on the supply order that had arrived that morning. He stopped himself, not wanting to upset Kate now.

"Do you remember going into the room?" Kate asked, her eyes searching his.

"I recall…" Nothing. He dug into his memory and a grain of recollection struck him. "The door was ajar. I was surprised. I remember that. When I walked in, I saw…two men." Adam's heart leaped in his chest with the vision. "Two men…one of them…"

Pain shot through his head, searing his thoughts. He grabbed his temple and closed his eyes, wanting to press back the pounding.

"Just lay still," Kate's voice soothed. "It'll come to you."

Fear tore through Kate's mind. "I'll get a cool cloth for your head." She headed into the bathroom and wet a washcloth, using the distraction to control her anxiety. She wrung out the excess water and returned to Adam.

He lay on his back, frustration written on his face.

"Here you go," she said, placing the cooling balm on his forehead.

A sound drew her attention to the doorway as Gordon Reese entered the room. He crossed to Adam's side. "Good to see you awake. Headache?"

Adam gave a faint nod.

"To be expected. You've had a bad concussion." He pulled up a chair and sat. "Do you want to hear the details now, or later?"

"Now," Adam said.

Gordon detailed the wounds Adam had received from the looting attempt and explained the chest tube, then the resulting surgery. When he asked for Adam's remembrance, he received the same news.

Brain damage? Fear filled Kate's mind. Could he have sustained permanent damage?

When Gordon Reese rose and stepped toward the door, Kate followed, determined to hear his opinion. "What's wrong?" she asked in the corridor outside Adam's room.

"I'm not sure, Kate, but my guess is he has retrograde amnesia."

She nodded. "That's what I feared. He doesn't remember what happened after he entered the dispensary."

"His memory may come back. Time will tell."

He walked away, and she stood there letting the thought weave through her.

Time would tell. Time would tell about so many things. How much time would pass before Kate faced the truth? She had to give up on her dreams of Adam. She imagined his touch, his lifesaving hands caressing her skin. She gazed at his lips, imagining his kisses. Foolish.

An impossible dream.

Adam had fallen asleep again as he had, on and off, since he'd awakened earlier. Kate looked at the doorway, hearing footsteps. Adam's parents hurried in, their eyes focused on their son.

Kate rose. "Just call his name. He'll wake up."

Liza's eyes brimming with tears, she inched forward as if afraid to touch him.

"Adam," Frank boomed, stepping to him without hesitation.

Adam's eyes shot open. He winced, then covered the expression with a faint grin. "Thought I recognized that voice, Dad." His gaze shifted. "Hi, Mom."

"Oh…Adam," she said, bending over to kiss his cheek. "We've been so worried."

Kate edged closer to the door. "I'll leave you for a while. I'll run down to the cafeteria."

Liza shook her head. "Adam, this young woman has been by your bed for days as faithful as a puppy. She's been so wonderful."

A grin spread across Adam's face. "What kind of puppy?"

Kate grimaced at Liza's well-meaning comment and gave them a wave as she left. Outside the door, she heard Liza scrambling to explain her comment. The longer Kate thought about the comparison, the more she agreed. She *had* been like a lovesick puppy—wagging her tail at the Montgomerys' attention and curling around the comfort of their kindness.

It was time she moved ahead with her life. Mooning over Adam was useless and would only cause her hurt and disappointment. Adam was a man out of her reach, and once his health improved, he'd be his old arrogant self again…although she'd even grown to accept that part of him.

She took the elevator to the first floor and made her way to the cafeteria. She'd lost weight since the ordeal. Her clothes hung on her, but food had lost its appeal. Being back home in Colorado Springs, she should have slid back into some semblance of normalcy. Next Monday she'd return to work and Colleen had agreed to take her soon to Adam's town house where she would have privacy and her own life back.

But did she want her old life to resurface? Her thoughts floated back to the Montgomerys. She'd grown fond of them both—Liza with her kindly ways, trying to be prim-and-proper while Frank blustered and made sandwiches out of his dinner, but both loved their children and gave their time and money to worthy causes…like Adam seemed to do. Kate liked that in them all.

Like? She admired them and wished she could be a part of their family….

Inside the cafeteria, Kate grabbed a salad plate and filled it with greens and other veggies. She sprinkled on some hard-boiled egg and bacon bits for a little protein, drizzled on the dressing, then added a glass of iced tea to her tray.

After paying the cashier, Kate made her way through the tables. When she spotted a familiar face, she gave a wave and joined her.

Dr. Emily Armstrong rose and opened her arms to Kate. "I heard you were back. What happened?"

Kate slid the tray on the table and embraced Emily. "You haven't heard the details? I thought everyone had."

"I was at a hematology conference last week. I just got back."

Emily returned to her chair, and Kate sat beside her. In a few words, she told Emily the gist of what had happened at the clinic while Emily grimaced at the details.

"It must have been horrible," she said, giving Kate's hand a squeeze. "How's Adam now?"

"Good, considering." Kate lifted her fork and paused. "But I'm worried. He has retrograde amnesia. I know that can correct itself, but I don't think they're sure if he's sustained any permanent brain damage. I'm heartsick. He's a wonderful plastic surgeon...and there are so many children who are born with birth defects. The need is so great in Venezuela."

Emily listened with interest. "Children are the ones who suffer in those poverty-stricken countries with poor nutrition and lack of medical treatment. It's heartbreaking, I agree."

"But despite the sadness and primitive conditions, the setting has its good points. It's beautiful there. You'd be amazed at the variety of flowers and birds, the coconut palms and the lagoon."

Emily grinned. "I can see it won you over. When I was married to Peter Vance, he always lived on the edge. He traveled to exotic places with so much danger. Even though we've been divorced for years, I remember how Peter loved excitement even when it meant his life might be in jeopardy...and I sat here with no adventurous spirit and no desire to put my life on the line for anything. Maybe I missed out on something."

"Maybe not. Some people aren't cut out for danger. Do you still hear from him?" Kate asked.

"Not in years. I have no idea where he is...and neither does his family. I recently asked his brother Sam and there's still no news."

Kate couldn't imagine caring about someone who

had vanished as Peter had done. "That's strange... and sad."

Emily gave a nod and became thoughtful.

"Our lives weren't always exciting in Santa Maria de Flores. It was quiet there—and safe, we thought— until that incident. We were busy and worked hard. Long hours often in the humidity and heat, but you got to know the people, especially the children. That made all the difference.

"That's why I specialize in pediatric hematology. I love kids. I'm sure the project is worthwhile." Emily gave a faint grin as if enjoying a private thought. "I can live without danger, but a little adventure might be interesting for a change."

Kate understood her smile. "They've pulled our team out for now, but I'm sure they'll send staff back again once this horrible incident is settled. To be honest, despite everything, I'd love to go back." *With Adam,* Kate added to herself.

"It's something to think about. Doctors Without Borders. It sounds unique. Intriguing."

Kate forked some salad, sensing she'd piqued Emily's interest. "You'd make a great contribution to the clinic with your skills."

"Thanks." She paused. "I'll have to drop by and see Adam. He and Peter were such good friends years ago," Emily said, returning to their earlier conversation. She took a bite of her sandwich and washed it down with a drink of soda. "So what about Lionel Valenti? That must have been horrible for him. Did he come back with you?"

"They held him there for questioning. I suppose

they wanted details. And he did kill someone, even though it was self-defense.''

Emily rolled her eyes. ''I hate to say it, but I've never thought of Lionel Valenti as the hero type.'' A sly grin settled on her mouth. ''But Adam. Now *that's* a different story.''

Her comment sent Kate's stomach reeling. ''Emily, don't tell me you have a thing for—''

''Me?'' Emily laughed. ''Not me, but I'd bet I know someone who does.''

Heat crept up Kate's neck as she tried to will it away. ''I'm his colleague and that's it. We spent months together, and I'm just concerned about him. It's natural.''

Part of Kate longed to unlock her heart and talk with Emily. Her friend had a good head on her shoulders, but to say her feelings aloud made them too real. ''You know Adam and I come from two different worlds. He's well-to-do and comes from a prestigious family in Colorado Springs. I'm… Well, I'm a nobody.''

''A nobody?'' Emily wagged her finger at Kate. ''Why would you say that? You're a respected nurse. You're talented and a beautiful woman. Any man would—''

''Any man, maybe, but not Mr. Attitude. I don't even think Adam likes me.''

Emily gave her a smug look. ''Time will tell, Kate.''

The phrase rang in her head. Kate had heard that before, but now it had so much more meaning.

Time will tell.

Chapter Seven

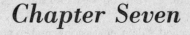

When Kate returned to Adam's room, his parents were gone. Adam lay on his back, his eyes closed, his face drawn. Her gaze was drawn to a large vase of flowers sitting on his bedstand.

Adam lifted his lids and watched her as she headed toward the bouquet. "Who sent the flowers?" she asked.

"A secret admirer."

Her heart twinged, and she wondered if he was serious. "No card?"

He gave her a pain-filled grin. "They're from my folks. They had them delivered."

His parents. The truth gave her an embarrassing kick. "They're beautiful." She shifted to his bedside and saw the discomfort etched in his face. "I know you're in pain. I'll check with the nurse and see if it's time for your meds."

"I'm miserable. I feel like cow droppings. Worse."

"You've had too much excitement today," she said.

"No. It's more than that."

His sharp voice caused her to falter. "Adam, I—"

As she turned, a stranger stood in the doorway. He gave her a questioning look. "I see you're awake." He sauntered into the room and stood beside Adam's bed.

"Hi, Sam. I woke up this morning. About time from what I hear."

She watched Adam put a congenial expression on his face, but it didn't fool Kate. He was miserable. Even so, he made the introductions.

"Sam Vance. Katherine...Darling."

Sam did a double take.

"It's my last name. Darling."

"Are you Adam's nurse?"

His scrutinizing look made her uneasy. "I'm a nurse, but I'm not Adam's—"

"Katherine worked with me in Venezuela as part of the Doctors Without Borders team. She found me when I was shot."

Sam's look seemed a quick study of her. "You were there?"

"Yes." Kate squirmed beneath his penetrating gaze.

"Sam's a detective with CSPD," Adam said.

"Detective?" Irritation ruffled up her spine. Was this official business? Kate thought he'd dropped by as a friend.

Sam drew over a chair, spun it around and straddled it, resting his hands on the back. "So you're okay?"

Adam shrugged. "I'm alive. I suppose that's good news."

"He's in a lot of pain," Kate said.

Sam gave Kate a glance, then returned his attention to Adam. "The department's anxious to know if you're up to talking."

"To you?" Adam asked, a frown settling on his face.

"Not me. I'm coordinating with the FBI."

Adam winced and shifted his head. "What do you mean, FBI?"

"The Feds are working with the authorities in Venezuela."

Adam closed his eyes and drew in a deep breath. "This stinks."

Sam recoiled at Adam's anger.

"It's not you. It's the pain. Ever had a hole in your gut?"

Kate twinged with his comment. She'd hoped Sam would back off. Adam needed rest, not questions.

"I'm sorry," Sam said.

Kate felt defensive. She stood above Adam's bed and smoothed his blanket. "Adam's not well. He really needs his pain medication. Couldn't you hold off until he's a little better?"

Pain wavered across Adam's face. "I know it's your job, but like Kate said, I'm hurting…and here's the bad news. I remember zilch."

Sam's head drew back like a cobra ready to strike. "Zilch? What do you mean?"

Kate swept in feeling like a defense attorney. "He means he remembers nothing. He has retrograde amnesia."

"Retro what?"

"I can't remember anything after I walked into the dispensary," Adam said.

When the frustration showed on Adam's face, Kate wanted to demand Sam leave him alone.

"Then you must have seen them," Sam said, leaning forward as if expecting a positive response.

"I remember seeing two figures—two men—but they're hazy. Shadows. No faces. Only…I keep thinking…" He slammed his fist into the mattress. "Forget it. I can't remember anything." He looked helplessly at Kate.

"He was alone when I found him," Kate said. "Cartons of drugs had been knocked onto the floor. Adam was right inside the entrance. I didn't see anyone and I don't know if Adam saw them, either. I'm sure Lionel Valenti gave them a description."

"Valenti?" Adam looked from Sam to Kate.

Seeing Adam's questioning gaze, Kate realized she hadn't told him the whole story. Sam listened with narrowed eyes.

"Is he still in Venezuela?" Adam asked.

"No," Kate said. "He dropped by to see you when you were still…unconscious. He looks terrible. And Dr. Eckerd dropped by a couple of times."

Adam looked discouraged. "Can you tell me anything, Sam? Any details about the guy Valenti shot? Who was he?"

Sam paused so long, Kate thought he hadn't heard Adam's question. Finally he ran a hand across his jaw and answered. "You know I can't jeopardize the case, Adam."

Though pain wracked Adam's face, he edged up

on an elbow. He pressed his hand against his chest. "This is my life, Sam. I should be able to know something about what happened." He dropped against the pillow.

Sam rose. "Sorry."

A grimace grew on Adam's face.

Kate recognized the symptom and knew he needed his pain medication. She moved to the call button and gave a push.

Adam frowned at her, but she ignored him and told the nurse what he needed when she answered.

Sam studied the two of them, his gaze shifting from one to the other, but Kate ignored him, too, and changed the subject. "What about the second guy? You can at least tell us if they nab him."

"Sorry. I can't."

"Sam, I wish—" Adam's words ended with a groan.

"I'll let the Feds know you're able to talk." He moved toward the doorway as if wanting to avoid seeing Adam's pain. "Just remember, Adam, justice will be served. We've been friends a long time, and a Vance never forgets. I'll do what I can to see those guys pay for what they've done."

When Sam vanished through the doorway, Adam looked at her with glazed eyes. She moved closer and leaned over his bed. "The meds should be here soon." She eyed the door again, wondering why the physician hadn't arrived. "Can you describe your sensations?"

"I don't know. Something's wrong."

Kate noticed perspiration beading his skin. "You

should be feeling better by now. Not great, but better.''

''You think I...can't handle pain?''

''No. I think you're sick.''

''Great deduction.''

She ignored his dig. He'd been pressed to the limit with his friend's questions.

Adam shuddered and dragged the blanket higher up his neck.

''Chills?''

He nodded, his eyes fluttering closed.

Chills and perspiration. A fever. She watched his breathing grow more labored every minute.

Fear rose up her back. She grasped his wrist and counted. His heartbeat pounded. Too rapid.

''I don't like this.''

Adam shifted his hand to his chest, his flesh growing as pale as death.

Kate leaned over again and pressed the nurse's call button.

He opened his eyes, and his glassy stare sent panic tearing through her.

''Get out of here and leave me alone.'' The words flew from his mouth, sharp and sudden as a jejen's sting.

Kate slumped with his attack, but the look on his face let her know this wasn't Adam talking. He was confused. Delirious. She'd never seen fear in his eyes before.

The nurse's voice questioned from the speaker.

Kate leaned closer. ''We need a doctor in here. Stat.'' A prayer flew as quickly to heaven.

Adam's face twisted in pain, and he gasped for air,

his chest rising and falling in fast unsteady pants. Hyperventilating.

She eyed the door. No doctor. She felt for Adam's pulse. His heart pounded. One-hundred eighty, she calculated.

Tachycardia.

She rammed the call button again. "Doctor! Stat!"

Dear Lord, please…please, help him.

He stood at the far end of the corridor and watched the drama unfold. Dr. Adam Montgomery, beloved plastic surgeon, had a life-threatening emergency. What a pity.

He pictured Montgomery strutting around with his self-importance—an arrogant snob, looking down his nose at those who didn't sit on his imperious throne.

Montgomery had never experienced poverty. He'd never known defeat. He'd grown up extremely privileged. And he pretended compassion in the name of Christianity. But today…today fate had sent Montgomery a deeper blow than the bullet that felled him. Missed its mark, in his opinion.

But one day nothing would save Montgomery. The precious plastic surgeon would no longer swagger past the fawning crowds who bowed and scraped. If he survived today, one day very soon, Montgomery wouldn't be as lucky. He would soon know defeat. Montgomery would experience the taste…of death.

Saturday morning, Adam saw his mother falter in the doorway while his father looked over her shoulder, their eyes focused on the IV pole beside him.

"What's wrong?" Liza asked, hurrying into the

room. Her gaze clung to the IV stand and bag hanging on its arm. "We miss seeing you one evening and—"

"I didn't want to worry you," Adam said.

Liza hovered above him. "Worry us? I would have been here, Adam. What is this?"

"Antibiotics."

"Now what?" his father asked, standing at the foot of his bed. "Infection?"

Adam nodded. "Sepsis. It's always a risk with an injury like I had." He pulled the blanket higher to thwart off the chill that assailed him. "They did a blood culture. That'll tell them what kind of bacteria."

"Is this negligence?" his father asked, his brows drawn into a frown. "If so—"

"It happens, Dad." Adam had no strength to argue with his father today. His mind was as muddied as the rutted mountain trails after rain.

His father smacked his hand on the bed railing, and Adam moaned with the jarring movement.

"Frank, be careful. Adam said these things happen." Liza's gaze returned to Adam. "We're just not happy that it happened to you." She brushed Adam's hair away from his face.

"I'm not happy ei—" His words faltered as Dr. Fletcher came through the doorway.

"Feeling better?" the internist asked.

Adam nodded, although at that moment he felt miserable.

Fletcher greeted Adam's parents, then turned to the patient. "Your blood culture identified the bacteria and your blood gases reveal acidosis. I've ordered a more aggressive antibiotic now that we know what we're fighting. I'm glad we caught it in time."

"Me, too," Adam said. "Any more surprises?"

Fletcher shook his head. "We've avoided septic shock and we'll keep a good watch that you don't develop bacterial pneumonia. That's good news, at least."

Tension charged through Adam's body. "When can I get out of here?"

"Once you're well. You're not ready yet."

Adam bit back his comment. Not ready yet? He was more ready than a child waiting for Christmas.

Kate came through the doorway. Adam lay with his arms folded behind his head, staring at the ceiling.

"Feeling better?"

He gave a faint nod, eyeing her over his blankets.

"What's up?" She stepped beside him.

"I'm thinking."

"That's progress," she said, pleased she could send him a barb before he gave one to her.

Though she could tell he fought it, a grin edged to his lips. "My, my."

"I learned that from the master," she said. She sank into the chair that stood beside his bed and gazed at him. Thankfulness covered her as she studied the brighter color in Adam's face and the familiar glint in his gorgeous eyes.

He didn't respond but stared back.

She watched him trace the line of her face with his gaze—her hair, her eyes, her lips and chin. The look sent her stomach on a spin.

"What are you thinking?" she asked.

"About you...for one."

"Me?" She shifted in the chair, caught by an uneasy feeling. "What about me?"

"My mother mentioned you'd been sitting here for days. I wondered why."

She felt uneasy with his question. How could she answer it? No matter what she might say, she knew the puppy-dog syndrome his mother had mentioned held some truth.

"I was worried," she said finally.

"And that's it?"

His gaze lingered on her face in a deep probing look that made her squirm.

"You don't understand, Adam. You weren't there." Her foolish comment made her grin. "Naturally you were there, but you were unconscious. You didn't see what I saw."

"I'm glad I wasn't there." He gave her a crooked grin.

Her good humor faded as the vision returned. "The horror of finding you bleeding on the floor...the terror I felt...I just can't forget it."

His expression darkened as he listened. His laugh lines deepened into a frown around his mouth. "Thanks for being there."

She gave him a wary look, waiting for the punch line.

"No. I mean it. You saved my life."

"No thanks needed. I thank God I was nearby."

Kate eyed his serious expression, the deep facial creases, and she longed to run her fingers over his growth of whiskers and feel his strong jaw beneath.

As if he realized, he shifted his hand and rubbed his chin. "What do you think?"

"I figured you're giving up doctoring to be a lumberjack." She felt pleased leaving the heavier topic.

"Not a bad idea after this experience." His smile flew away as quickly as it had appeared, and he slapped his hand against the sheet and gestured to the IV pole. "I hate this. I'm not supposed to be lying here. I'm a doctor, not a patient."

Kate numbed at his sudden anger. "Right now, you're a patient, and if you relax and cooperate, you'll be up and out of here soon. For all your injuries and now sepsis, you're doing well."

"Well? That's because you're not here—" he poked the sheet "—in this bed. Try being here feeling helpless. I can't even shave with this thing." He gave a tug at his IV tubing.

"Be careful. You'll jerk that IV out and then they'll have to start poking again." She moved in closer to check the needle. It looked fine to her.

His wide emotional swings were part of his injury, but she found it irritating. "You want a shave? I'd be happy to oblige." She rose and headed for the supplies before he could say no.

When she returned, she carried a disposable razor and shaving cream. She stopped in the rest room and filled a basin with warm water, then headed back to Adam.

"You're not shaving me." He pulled his head as far back as he could in a prone position.

"I'm not? Why?"

"You look too gleeful with that razor."

She eyed the blade and laughed. "Not a bad idea.

I've given that some thought on occasion, but not since we've been back.''

He looked defeated. "I know. I look helpless."

Before he could stop her, she dampened his face and covered his jaw and neck with the shaving cream. While he winced, she pulled the razor along his whiskers, enjoying the closeness, the almost intimate feeling.

As the beard vanished, his cheeks felt soft against her hand as she followed the strong contour of his jawline. She listened to the bristles scrape as she removed the beard from his neck with a gentle upward stroke.

Their nearness awakened her senses. She averted her eyes, but he lifted his hand and drew her chin around to face him. His look made her weak.

Kate fought the sensation.

"You've been so kind…and sweet," he said, brushing his fingers along his clean-shaven jaw.

Kate eased back and rinsed the excess cream from his face, heady from the herbal scent and Adam's closeness. When she had finished, she tilted the mirror on his bed tray to let him look.

"Not bad," he said, capturing her gaze. "If you ever give up nursing, you could be a barber. I'll be happy to give you a reference."

Kate raised an eyebrow and lowered the mirror, but before she pulled her hand away, Adam captured it in his. He didn't speak, and she couldn't. He carried her hand to his cheek and pressed it against his skin. Her heart swelled and rose to her throat. Her pulse thundered until she feared he would hear it.

"Smooth?"

She could only nod.

"Thank you, Katherine."

His attention was more than she could handle, and Kate pulled her hand away, praying she could contain the emotion that boiled through her limbs. "You're welcome," she murmured.

Struggling with her feelings, she rose and grabbed the basin. As she stepped toward the doorway, she saw Colleen standing in the threshold, watching them.

She darted past her to empty the water and to hide her embarrassment. Colleen had been watching them from the doorway, and her grin made Kate uncomfortable.

Kate listened to their conversation from the bathroom. She looked at herself in the mirror and saw a flush on her cheeks. Her feelings had become too obvious. She'd become overly protective. Adam was feeling better. She should back off...but she couldn't.

Kate swished the basin under the water, wiped her hands and stepped back into the room.

Colleen swung around, a look of surprise on her face. "I wondered where you'd gone."

"Just emptying the basin," she said, sinking into a chair.

Colleen left the foot of the bed and sat beside Adam on the corner of the mattress. "I just stopped by to see how you're doing."

Adam flung his arms to his sides. "Take a look."

"Not bad. Looks like you have a fresh shave." She sent Kate a grin.

"He was getting prickly," Kate said, trying to ease her discomfort.

Adam tousled Colleen's short spiky hair. "Don't you need a haircut?"

"Speak for yourself." She mussed his dark curly locks. "Anyway, I'm also here for Kate. We're heading for your town house." She faltered a moment. "Mom told you?"

Adam nodded, and Kate realized his pain had grown noticeably worse than before. "The folks have an extra key."

Colleen reached into her pocket and dangled it in front of him. "I have your car key, too. She might as well use that sleek silver sports car of yours."

A look of panic rose in Adam's eyes, but the pain washed it away, and he sank deeper into the mattress without a comment.

"See," Colleen said, "he's in total agreement. Ready?" She rose and took a couple steps toward the door.

Kate lifted a finger. "One minute, okay? I want to go check on a couple things before I leave."

"Sure. No hurry," Colleen said. She stepped closer to Adam's bed. "The longer I've been here the more rotten you look. Can I do anything?"

Adam shook his head, wishing everyone would just leave him alone, but that was his pain talking. "No. I'll be fine once I get my pills." He closed his eyes, willing away the driving ache that seemed to pulse through his body.

Colleen sank to the edge of the bed again and patted Adam's shoulder. "From what I saw, I think you're doing fine right now...if you get my drift."

"Cut the jokes. I'm miserable." He opened his eyes and caught a grin glinting in Colleen's eyes.

"Can't be miserable with Kate around. You're not fooling me, you know. How long has this been going on?"

"What?" Adam sorted through her comment, trying to make sense out of it. "What's going on?"

"I'm your sister, Adam. It's obvious. Kate's been sitting here day in and out, worrying about you. You don't think she's here to collect your life insurance, do you? She's crazy about you."

"You're out of your mind." Adam said the words, but the truth hung over him like a beacon. "Get out of here and let me suffer in peace."

Colleen chuckled and backed away. "I know you've had some memory loss, but you're not blind, brother. You'd better take a good look."

"Good look at what?" Kate asked, coming into the room. "By the way, they said they're on the way with your meds. I'll see you later."

Colleen linked her arm in Kate's, gave a wave and steered Kate through the doorway without answering.

Adam heard her chuckle echo from the hallway.

Finally alone, Adam rolled with the pain throbbing in his chest. His mind muddied with his misery, but Colleen's words tumbled through him and pulsated as deep as the pain.

Kate?

His mind flew back to the days before the shooting. He'd enjoyed Kate from afar, fearing if he let himself admit the growing feelings, he'd be lost.

He admired her nursing skills. She showed wisdom and intelligence working with patients. Her compassion and control amazed him. On long days when his composure had stretched its limit, Kate stayed calm and collected.

She was a beauty, too. Beautiful inside and out. He'd thought so from day one. But she'd always seemed standoffish, and he'd probably encouraged it with his attitude. He'd strutted around the clinic with his self-importance that built a barrier between him and the truth. What was he trying to hide? Why was he afraid to let the real Adam Montgomery be seen?

He'd been flawed from childhood with his preoccupation with things. He'd made his microscopes and lab equipment his friends and had avoided people. Sure, he'd had competition. A good-looking brother and a feisty sister who'd made life wonderfully difficult. His father had expected the best, and he'd worked hard to be the best. He had reached his goal. He was a respected plastic surgeon, but he'd lost something in the process. His humanity…or at least, his sociality.

Still he and Kate had enjoyed some good times together. He remembered how lovely she'd been the evening they'd watched the sunset together—the orange sun sinking to coral and spreading on the horizon; the canopy of color spewing warm highlights in her blond hair.

And the lagoon. They'd laughed that day when he'd been frightened by an animal in the brush. He'd jumped back and tripped over himself trying to get away. They'd joked about the mangroves that appeared to be taking a walk through the swamp on their long gangling roots. Silly things filled his mind.

But he'd held back. He'd called her Katherine

while everyone called her Kate—a stupid way to try to control his feelings.

He pictured her sitting in the chair by the window the day he'd wakened. He'd thought her an angel…and maybe she was. She'd watched over him day and night according to everyone. But why was she there? Did she revel in seeing him humbled and defenseless? Was this only another example of Kate's compassion and kindness?

Or could Colleen be right?

Chapter Eight

Colleen's SUV flew along Union Boulevard past Colorado Springs Country Club and Palmer Park. Kate saw the town houses from the highway with Austin Bluffs in the background. Colleen turned off the highway and wound the vehicle through the streets until she slowed and pulled along the curb.

Kate got out and gazed at the three-story gray buildings with wide windows to offer a view of the surrounding mountains and the lush green of the park. The view filled her with a sense of freedom. When Kate shut the passenger door, Colleen rounded the car and tossed her the house keys.

Kate clutched them as they headed up the walk, her heart fluttering at the thought of living—albeit temporarily—in Adam's home. She turned the key and pushed open the door.

Inside, Kate faltered, gazing at the expansive rooms. She could have put her old apartment inside the living room. "It's great," she said to Colleen.

"Mom and I decorated it. If we'd left it to Adam, he would have lived with the white walls and hand-me-down furniture. Sometimes I think Adam has no class."

Kate felt her jaw sag at Colleen's comment. Adam was pure class in Kate's opinion. She let her gaze travel over the neutral walls with a rich navy sofa and burgundy draperies. The wide window in front offered a wonderful view of the park, and when Kate turned, she saw the foothills from the back window.

She thought of her own small apartment, which looked onto a parking lot and the side of another building. So much for scenery. Her shoulders rose as Kate envisioned the two different lifestyles. She was longing for the impossible.

"Let me show you around," Colleen said, motioning her to follow.

Kate walked behind her through an attractive dining room and into the kitchen.

"Adam never entertains," Colleen said. "He uses the kitchen to make coffee. Instant probably." She flashed Kate a smile.

"Follow me." She hurried on ahead, and Kate tagged behind up the stairs.

Colleen led her to a bedroom and chuckled when she saw Kate's reaction.

"I love it," Kate said, walking into a room with a tulip border and ruffled toss pillows. "How did you manage this?"

Colleen grinned. "We tricked him."

Kate wandered to the window and admired the same lovely view of the park.

"This is yours. The bathroom's in the hall. The

room next door is Adam's office. You can snoop around there when you need something to put you to sleep. The walls are white.''

Kate loved Colleen's feisty sense of humor. With all the comments, Kate could see the love in her eyes for Adam.

When they returned downstairs, Colleen showed her Adam's gym in the walkout basement and the below-ground-level garage housing the sports car.

.''It's a stick shift,'' Colleen said.

''I can handle it.'' Kate added, ''I think,'' to herself. She hadn't driven a stick in years.

''I have your bags from my folks' house in the trunk. I'll bring them in. Then I have to run. I have an interview for that feature I told you about.''

''How's it going?''

Colleen nodded. ''I wasn't getting anywhere at first, but then I found a couple of women willing to open up. It's turning out to be more than I expected. I think Sam and my editor will be happy.''

''Good for you,'' Kate said.

Kate joined Colleen outside, and in moments her bags were upstairs. As she looked around the tulip-bordered room, reality settled over her. She was in Adam's home and faced with a kind of intimacy that rocked her.

After Colleen said goodbye, Kate sank into the plush sofa and gazed through the window at the rugged park with cactus and piñon pines lining the trail. The blue sky feathered with clouds rested against the rolling landscape, sending her heart on a wavering journey. Being in Adam's home, she inhaled a musky scent she'd come to recognize as his.

Kate pushed her hand against her heart, realizing how foolish she was to allow herself to imagine a relationship with him. She had nothing to offer. He had everything.

As Kate surveyed the masculine luxury, truth hit home again harder than before. Adam was not only a self-made man, but stemmed from a family with status and expectations. She'd become a lowly nurse who worked her way through college and who inherited nothing from her past except memories. Sad memories.

Shame filled Kate as her thoughts probed the past. Her mother had done the best she could. Kate knew she should be grateful for her Christian upbringing. That was one thing that held her fast and it was a gift no one could take away from her.

Pride. Vanity. They had no place in her life. She'd done the best she could with what she had and wasn't going to let Adam Montgomery and his privileged background make her feel any different.

"I am worthy," she said aloud, but her mind told her it wasn't so.

Adam opened his eyes and saw the angel. Kate sat in the chair by the window, the light shining through her hair as it had the day he'd first awakened from his injury, but this time she wore a bright red top that warmed her fair skin and sent color to her cheeks. The color licked his senses like flames in the hearth, warming him and taunting him with dangerous thoughts.

He watched her in silence, her head lowered, her fingers turning the pages of a paperback. How many hours had she made a vigil at his bedside? His own personal angel. The thought made him grin.

He turned on his side, forgetting his IV, and pain jabbed his arm while another throb rolled through his stomach. He couldn't contain the moan that bellowed from his throat.

Kate flew to his side like an arrow. Bull's-eye. She had her hand on his arm, helping him to settle back against the mattress and the irritating sheets that kept him mummified.

Adam wanted freedom. He wanted to escape this sterilized beige-walled prison that had once been his safe haven when he was well and caring for his own patients. Now he was one, too.

And it had been too long. About the time he'd begun to make headway with the bullet wound, the infection took over.

"I hate this place." His head bounced back against the pillow, jarring him again. "I don't even know what day it is."

"It's still Saturday. All day."

He gave her a fiery look. "I need to do something. Walk. I don't care about pain or IV needles. I'll never get my strength back if I don't move."

Kate shook her head and shrugged. "Great idea. I'll help you. Just let me check with the nurse."

He swallowed his demand as she left, realizing he'd just initiated his own torture.

In a moment, Kate returned with a walker and slid it toward him. "I think this is the right height for you."

"Forget it. I'm not using a walker." His pride soared, but Kate didn't flinch.

"Yes, you are. And they have orders to get you up

today anyway, so you'd be doing it whether you wanted to or not.''

Adam witnessed color rising in her cheeks and the spirited way she flitted around him…as if she were in charge. No one controlled Adam Montgomery. The words smacked against his head like a mallet. His shoulders sagged, and Adam faced the truth.

He had no control over his life at this moment. The hospital…and the good Lord were in charge. He whispered a thankful prayer that God had been on his side or he'd be walking with real angels and not the one tempting him with her tight red top and smug smile.

Kate helped him ease to the edge of the bed and slid a robe up one arm, then draped the other side over the shoulder of the arm that had the IV. He had no desire to prance around the hospital corridors with his backside on display.

Before he stood, a nurse came through the doorway. ''Here's your pain meds. You'll want them before you walk.''

He longed to knock them out of her hand to prove he didn't need anything or anyone, but reality struck him. As his father always said, cockiness in this situation would be cutting off his nose to spite his face.

Adam took the pills and accepted the paper cup of water. He swilled it down and watched the nurse leave the room.

Kate hovered nearby, steadying the walker. Her amber eyes taunted him as she watched him lean forward to lift his weight.

Adam gripped the walker, frustrated with the whole situation. He felt helpless and vulnerable for the first time in his life. He hated the feeling. Weakness overcame him, and he stood a moment to catch his breath.

"I can't take another minute of this. I'm tired of being helpless and—"

"God doesn't promise us a life without pain or suffering," Kate said, her face so close to his as she clung to the other side of the walker. "The Lord promises to be there when we need Him." Her eyes filled with sadness, and the look confused him. "Have you asked God for help?"

Shame poured over Adam like a rainstorm. He'd been so busy feeling sorry for himself, he'd forgotten about God's mercy.

Kate put her cool palm against his hand. "You don't have to count on yourself or on anyone. Only the Lord. My favorite verses from Second Corinthians say, 'Rather, as servants of God we commend ourselves in every way: in great endurance; in troubles, hardships and distresses; sorrowful, yet always rejoicing; poor, yet making many rich; having nothing, and yet possessing everything.' I've tried to live by those words, Adam."

Her words startled him. "You remembered all of that?"

A faint smile curved her mouth. "Do you remember your address? Your telephone number?"

He nodded, wondering if she'd flipped out. What did that have to do with anything?

"The scripture is more important than either of those. It guides our feet down a different path. One that's lasting. Those verses have saved my life…at least, my sanity."

He thought a moment, his curiosity aroused by her

last statement, but also, the deeper meaning of what she'd said. Adam didn't ask questions. He sensed she would resent his prying. Instead, he leaned forward, hoping to raise himself with her help.

Kate stood back, giving him space to get accustomed to the walker. When he felt confident, he slid his feet forward, weakness buckling his knees. He clung to the support with a death grip and eased his way to the door with Kate beside him pushing his IV stand.

As they moved, Kate's body brushed against his when he swayed. He could smell her sweet aroma—flowers and sun, a fragrance that drew him back to Santa Maria de Flores. Her heels tapped against the tile, matching the rhythm of his heart. Awareness ran down his arms. So close, yet so distant in many ways. He barely knew her.

He crept down the corridor a few doorways, then stopped to catch his breath. "I feel like a child learning to walk."

"It takes time. Don't be discouraged." She squeezed his good arm. "You've been through so much."

"I think I'll go back," he said.

She didn't argue, and he inched around and shuffled back, angered with each step. Anger or fear?

He paused to calm his irritation and a thought struck him. "Did I tell you the FBI showed up before you got here?"

She shook her head. "Was it awful?"

"No, but they weren't thrilled I couldn't remember any details. I had to explain it to them six times."

"Persistence solves crime, I suppose."

He managed to move his body forward again. "I have to admit they were thorough."

When they'd reached his room, he crumpled onto the bed. Kate helped him remove the robe, and he sank backward.

"A little each day, Adam. It'll become easier."

He noted her concerned expression. His guardian angel. She'd even reminded him to pray, which he hadn't even thought of. It was time he asked for the Lord's help.

Unbidden, he grasped her hand and pulled her closer. "You're a beautiful woman inside and out, Kate Darling."

She drew back, her surprised expression shifting to a frown.

Her reaction startled him.

"You're delirious," she said, and stepped away.

He was. Deliriously falling for Kate.

His skin prickled as he passed Montgomery's room. He'd seen him shuffling down the corridor with a walker, and it made his heart feel good to see the man miserable. Seeing Montgomery's confidence as shaky as his weakened legs filled his heart with triumph. The only element that spoiled the picture was his very private nurse who seemed glued to his side.

He'd noticed the two earlier, and he wasn't stupid. For years, Montgomery had turned a blind eye to pretty women, but the Darling nurse—he cackled at his private, little joke—had chopped away at the mighty Montgomery defenses. That was almost as good as what he had in store.

A plan was what he had needed—a plan to rid the

*world of Montgomery and save his own neck. He'd
researched and scrutinized until he had it down to the
minute. He knew which nurses took breaks when. He
knew what a doctor's orders could accomplish...even
if he wasn't the doctor. He grinned to himself at the
luscious idea he'd conceived...and it would work. No
one would know who or what, but him.*

"*Your day is coming, Montgomery,*" he muttered.

When Adam's parents arrived, Kate took a break.
She wandered to the cafeteria, but instead of eating
there, she bought a tuna sandwich and soda and
headed outside to a park bench in one of the court-
yards.

Kate wasn't in the mood to talk to anyone. Her
mind had weighted with concern as she observed
Adam's pain and weakness. He could have a low pain
threshold, but she didn't think so. He'd been tough in
Venezuela, not admitting the sting of the jejen flies
or rarely complaining about the other discomforts of
the village.

The worry weighted her spirit while she added another concern. He'd called her Kate. Adam had never
done that. Not once. Today he'd told her she was
beautiful and called her Kate.

She could still feel his hand against hers. He'd captured her fingers before she knew what was happening. She'd almost let herself believe her dream had
come true. She wanted to stay there, palm against
palm, to feel his pulse beat against hers, to feel flesh
against flesh. Why had he done that?

Kate didn't think of Adam as a game player. He'd
always been direct and unflattering. He'd spoken his

piece. She was a good nurse, but not good for much else. He'd told her that often. Why now? Why when she felt so tempted to let herself fall in love?

Fight against the emotion. The words rose like a mission statement. She had to be her own cheerleader, rallying herself to be strong and to win the battle. Battle? She needed to retain her self-esteem. Adam could be toying with her. He'd admitted he was bored and frustrated. He wanted action. He wanted to escape. Toying with her could be a means of mental distraction for him.

But would Adam do that?

The question rolled through her thoughts like loose marbles, banging against one another with little clinks, nudging one thought away and letting another bounce closer to the truth. Truth. She didn't know it anymore.

The sandwich seemed to clog in her throat. Kate swallowed, forcing herself to eat for sustenance, not pleasure. She sipped the soda, letting it wash away the tuna. With it half-eaten, she rose and dropped it in the trash can. Later when her mind wasn't so agitated, she'd try again to get something into her stomach.

She pondered going home…but home was Adam's house. There or here, her mind filled with him. Images of their time together, thoughts of him today lying in pain on the hospital bed and visions of the future—imaginings she was even afraid to dream.

Kate had more distractions at the hospital than at Adam's town house so she took the elevator to the surgical floor. In two more days, she'd be back to work. She needed the routine to keep her head on straight. On Monday she would feel normal again.

Frank Montgomery's voice drifted into the hallway, and Kate girded a smile before she stepped into the room. Liza had drawn the chair beside the bed while Frank paced at the foot, his arms flailing with mayoral issues that registered in Kate's mind in bits and pieces.

"Frank, sit here," Liza said. "Your pacing is making me nervous."

She rose, but Frank stayed where he was. Liza admitted defeat and moved to Kate's side.

"How are you doing, dear? Is Adam's place comfortable enough for you?"

Kate grinned. "It's more than comfortable. It's a lovely spot. What a view! You and Colleen decorated it so nicely. I'm very happy there."

"I'm glad. And his car? Does it drive well?"

"Very nice. Better than my clunker." Kate gave Adam a smile but would have given a bundle to have her junker back. She pictured herself jerking out of Adam's garage and down the driveway like a new driver. Though she drove to the hospital that morning without incident, she still didn't have the hang of the manual transmission. Maybe that's why she dreaded going back to the town house. If she waited until evening, the traffic would be lighter.

Frank's voice rose in a tirade to Adam about some political issue, and Liza drew her aside.

"You've been such a good friend these past days. Not just to Adam but to all of us. Would you join me for lunch tomorrow? Right after church, perhaps."

A chill rushed along Kate's spine. "Lunch? I—I haven't been—"

"Whatever time's good for you. Where do you worship? If the service is later, we can work around that."

"That's not the problem," Kate said, trying to decide what the problem was. "I usually attended Community Church, but—"

"You've just returned home, I know. Well, you're welcome to worship with us anytime you'd like. We attend Good Shepherd Christian Church."

"Thank you," Kate said, wondering about Liza's motivation.

"How about Sunday one o'clock for lunch? Would that work? We'll eat at the country club. It's not far from Adam's town house. Right at Union and Templeton Gap Road."

"The country club?" Her stomach tightened. "Yes, I know where that is."

"Wonderful. Then you'll join me there tomorrow?"

"That'll be wonderful," Kate said, grinding her teeth to hold herself from making an excuse. And why? Liza meant nothing but kindness, and Kate had enough social graces to enjoy a country-club luncheon.

"Time to go," Frank said, checking his watch. "You're in our prayers, son. We have some kind of shindig tonight that your mother roped me into, but I'll come by tomorrow sometime."

"That's fine, Dad," Adam said, propping his head upward on his folded arms.

"Mind the nurses," Liza said, bending over to kiss

him on the cheek. "I'm so pleased to see you look more lively."

Kate wanted to attest to his liveliness, but she only waved her goodbye as they left, leaving her and Adam staring at each other from across the room.

Adam patted the chair. "Come and sit beside me."

Kate looked at him while her thoughts presented a rebuttal. *No. Never. I can't sit close to you.* While the words pelleted her mind, her feet propelled her forward like someone hypnotized. She sank next to him and studied his face, longing to ask him the meaning of his actions.

"I've come to think of you as my guardian angel, Kate."

"It's only an illusion," she said, hoping to discourage his pursuing the topic.

"I'll admit, you've surprised me. Here you are every day more dedicated to a patient than I've ever seen. I thought you hated the ground I walked on…but I'm seeing a different side of you. You're compassionate and faithful…not to mention full of charm, intelligence and beauty."

She felt a frown burrow onto her face, and she wanted to recoil from his wonderful words—words she'd never heard anyone say.

Adam slid his hand over hers and caressed it, moving as slowly as a summer breeze. With each shift of his fingers, Kate's pulse jolted like a wild colt. She longed to pull her hand away as she'd done earlier, but the feeling wrapped around her heart and kept her immobile.

"I never appreciated you, Kate…not all of you. I

admired your nursing skills. I told you that, but you're so much more and—''

''Adam.''

As if struck by lightning, Kate and Adam yanked apart at the interruption.

Chapter Nine

Kate recognized Dr. Valenti's voice before she saw him. "Lionel," she said, straightening her back and stepping away from Adam.

His gaze shifted between her and Adam. "How are you?" He sauntered into the room. "I've been trying to see you, but you were still out of it. How's it going?"

"Forgive me for not standing," Adam said, giving him a wry look. "As you can see, I'm a little under the weather."

"I know." He stepped closer to the foot rail. "And I've heard you have—"

"Amnesia," Adam said before he could.

"Retrograde amnesia. The doctors are hopeful he'll retrieve his memory." Kate wished she could control her urge to be Adam's protector.

"Then that's good news," Valenti said. He released the railing and tucked his hands into his pockets. "Do you recall anything at all?"

"Nothing. Zilch," Adam said, a frown furrowing his face. "It's frustrating. What happened to you?"

"I was detained in—"

"I know about that. I meant that day. What happened?"

Lionel jingled the coins in his pockets. "It was dreadful. I remember hearing something. A backfire, I thought, but I didn't see anything through the window so I decided to check it out. As I reached the clinic, I bumped into two men barreling out the door. They were running, and I saw the gun."

"You must have been petrified," Kate said, imagining how she would have felt meeting them in the hallway.

"I didn't have time to think. The one shot past me, but I ran smack into the other. His head butted against my lip, but I struggled to stay on my feet. He had the gun. I surprised him, I guess. I grabbed his wrist and twisted. The gun went off and got him in the chest. He fell to the ground. It's all a blur."

"I'm glad you weren't injured," Adam said.

Lionel Valenti scrutinized Adam's face. "So why amnesia? The shot missed your head."

"I fell and hit the corner of that cabinet by the door."

Kate heard irritation in Adam's voice and wondered if he would blow up again. His emotions swayed like a windsock in a storm.

Lionel Valenti frowned. "I'm surprised you don't remember anything from before you fell."

"Well, I don't." Adam's tone rose in volume.

Kate moved forward and rested her hand on his

arm. "Adam was unconscious until yesterday. He needs time to heal."

"Sorry. I figured if you recognized one of them they could get the thing solved, and we'd all get back to normal. I'm sure everyone wants to return to the clinic."

"No, it's me," Adam said. "I'm just tired of people telling me what I should remember. I don't recall a thing, and it's frustrating."

"I understand." Lionel Valenti's head drooped. "It's been difficult for all of us."

Adam drew back and studied him. "I hate to say this, man, you look worse than I do. You're right. We all need to get back to normal."

Lionel drew up his shoulders. "It's hard to get back to normal when you've been through what I have. I realize you have your problems, but I've had my own ordeal. I was interrogated and grilled for hours in the flea-infested city jail...as if *I* were the criminal. That's not easy to forget."

Adam slumped against the pillow and rubbed his eyes. "I heard. It must have been awful."

"It was." Lionel Valenti gestured to the IV. "And now you have sepsis, I hear." He paused a moment, staring at Kate, and his face twitched. "Nice to have your own private nurse."

"I work on this floor," Kate said, not liking his implication.

Lionel gave her a knowing look. "Right." He lifted his hand. "I need to get back to work. Take care, Adam."

Before either could say goodbye, he'd scooted through the doorway.

Kate gave Adam an unspoken reprimand, and he nodded as if he understood. Adam's self-control had been as wounded as his chest.

She sank into the chair again, wondering what Lionel Valenti had thought seeing them together. She wished he hadn't.

Kate clamped her teeth together to keep from gaping. The Colorado Springs Country Club was as elegant as she had imagined. The central foyer, adorned with a lavish deep-toned tapis carpet, featured a round Chippendale table holding a lavish bouquet in a Japanese urn. The wide molding and rich wood accents lent opulence to the setting.

To the left, a delectable aroma greeted Kate, and she was drawn forward. Waiting for service, she stood in the doorway of the dining room and gazed at the deep inset ceiling with ornate white cornices above the creamy yellow walls.

Liza was already seated and the maître d' led Kate across the thick burgundy-and-green carpet to Liza's table at a window looking out at the lush lawn of the golf course.

The waiter pulled out a chair and Kate sat, slipping the white cloth napkin onto her lap. "This is lovely," she said to Liza.

"No trouble finding it, I hope."

"Not at all." Kate lifted the menu the maître d' had left behind and perused it. The prices nearly made her eyebrows shoot upward, but she maintained decorum and was grateful she was Liza's guest.

When they'd mulled over their choices and placed their order, Kate handed the waiter her menu, then folded her hands and waited for Liza to begin the conversation.

Liza took a sip of water with lemon, then grinned. ''I suppose you know I have an ulterior motive.''

Her words racked through Kate like fingernails on a chalkboard. ''I wondered.''

''I truly wanted to show my appreciation for all you've done for Adam. You've been a faithful friend.''

Kate clasped her hands together in a death grip. ''Allowing me into your home and loaning me Adam's town house and car is enough thanks, Mrs. Montgomery.''

''Please, dear, call me Liza.''

Kate had always called her Liza in her thoughts, but hesitated being overly familiar with Adam's mother. ''Thank you. I'll do that.''

Liza took a roll from the basket and smothered it with herbed butter. The inviting scent drifted across the table. She shifted the bread toward Kate. ''Try one while they're warm.''

She followed Liza's direction and sank her teeth into the luscious crescent.

''You have great compassion, Kate. I've been thinking about our upcoming fund-raiser. I wondered if you might volunteer to help.''

''Fund-raiser?'' Kate's mind went blank. She hadn't heard of a fund-raiser for the hospital, and one for the country club seemed ludicrous.

''For the shelter. The Galilee Women's Shelter. I mentioned it to you a few days ago.''

''Yes, you did. I'd forgotten.'' She lifted her water glass and took a sip, moistening her dry mouth and hoping to give herself time to think. "What type of volunteering did you need?"

"We have a guest list and we'll be getting together invitations. We always need help stuffing envelopes and putting on labels, making telephone calls. So many things. Please don't feel you have to do this. I just thought that—"

"I'm very interested in women's shelters." The admission surprised Kate. Her heart ached, thinking of the women and children in need. "I'd be happy to do what I can. Many women would be lost without a place like the shelter." The words caught in her throat.

"It *is* a worthwhile project. That's why I give them my time."

And money, Kate added to herself. "When would you need me?"

"I'll give Jessica Mathers your name. She's the development director for the Galilee facility and a wonderful woman. She does so much promotion and fund-raising. They'd be lost without her."

"Certainly. Give her my name…and you can keep me posted."

"Thank you, dear," Liza said. "You're always so kind. Do you know where the shelter's located?"

"On Galilee Avenue."

"That's right."

Silence hovered over them, and Kate watched Liza's face, knowing she had more to say. The woman shifted her water glass and lined up her silverware until she stopped and paused a moment.

"I'm curious," Liza said, looking directly into Kate's eyes. "I've waited so long to see my children settled and happily married…and I'm still waiting. I've noticed something going on between you and Adam, and I was hoping you would give me a reason to be happy. Adam is so closemouthed about his private life.''

Kate had expected as much. She ignored her pounding heart and struggled to keep her voice calm. "I'm sorry to disappoint you, Mrs—Liza. Adam and I are, at best, friends."

"But…you've been so attentive, so concerned. Devoted, really, and I thought—"

Kate shook her head. "Friends." She watched disappointment settle on the woman's face.

"Is it you or Adam?"

"I'm sorry?" Kate said, not sure what the woman was asking.

"Are you the one holding back or is it Adam? You may be fooling each other, but a mother sees the truth. I'm certain your feelings are greater than friendship."

Kate reached across the table and touched Liza's hand. "I'm very fond of you and your family. And I'm fond of Adam. We spent a great deal of time together in Venezuela…not only in the clinic, but we shared living quarters with common rooms. We ate meals together. When you spend that much time with someone, you learn to care about them."

Liza lowered her head. "I'd only hoped that perhaps I was right. My son's face brightens when you come into the room. I've seen it more than once. He doesn't express his emotions often, but—"

"I think he's grateful. He keeps reminding me that I saved his life, which isn't totally true, but I was there." Kate wrestled with the truth, wanting to admit

to the woman why she had to harness her feelings.
She could never tell them—especially Adam—about
her childhood and poverty. "Your family and mine
come from different worlds. I really am no match for
the history and contribution your family has here in
Colorado Springs...nor do I have your resources."

"My dear, history and contribution do not make
the person. It's a happening. A circumstance. God is
the center of our lives. He is what's important. Remember the verse in Proverbs. 'Rich and poor have
this in common: The Lord is the Maker of them all.'"

"Yes. I know that verse well."

The conversation halted as the waiter presented
their meals. Kate paused to calm her ragged nerves.
Liza's probing had set her on edge...and she sensed
Liza had more on her mind.

But what? She had no idea.

Adam tried to hold a conversation with his parents,
but he struggled to concentrate. Other things pressed
on his mind. He felt stronger after a few days of the
IV therapy, and he'd escaped septic shock and pneumonia. He hadn't avoided, however, having his heart
captured by a woman who didn't seem to give a hoot
about him.

Since Kate's return to her nursing position, he'd
missed her even though she worked on his floor. For
the past two days, she'd seemed to ignore him. The
whole situation puzzled him. He found himself watching the corridor, hoping to see Kate flit past.

Seeing a flash of white outside the doorway, he
watched, hoping Kate would drop by. Disappointment
settled in when a young nurse hurried past.

No Kate.

His mother caught his look and followed his gaze. "Where's Kate today?"

"She's busy with other patients." He tried to hide his dejection. "She's back working on the floor now."

"Yes, she told me. We had a very nice lunch on Sunday," Liza said.

"Who?"

"Kate and I."

"You and Kate had lunch? Where?"

"At the country club. We had a lovely talk."

Adam held his breath. His mother was a born matchmaker and the thought made him more uncomfortable than the sepsis that had wracked his body.

"Kate's agreed to help out with the Galilee Women's Shelter fund-raiser."

"Fund-raiser." Adam's spirit lifted for a fleeting moment. He knew his mother too well to think it had stopped there. Concern spiked his flash of comfort. "You took her to lunch to talk about the fund-raiser. That's it?"

Her face brightened with a telling smile. "Naturally, we talked about you."

Adam gave his father a pleading look, but Frank only shrugged.

"Naturally." His heart sank and Kate's recent change in attitude fell into place. "And what did you discuss about me?"

Looking at his mother's face, he knew in his gut she'd gone too far again. "You didn't ask her how she felt about me, did you?"

She didn't respond for a moment. "Not exactly."

"Mother, will you learn not to get involved—?" A tremor raced over his limbs, and he felt perspiration bead on his forehead. He swallowed his misery and continued. "When will you learn not to get involved in our lives? If Kate had feelings for me, you'd scare her away." And that's what had happened. He knew it.

Frank stirred, pacing to the windows and back. "Liza, you know how the children feel. Why do you keep trying to marry them off?"

"Because," she said, her voice rising in defense, "Adam is fond of Kate. I see it. I'm his mother, and I know these things."

Adam opened his mouth, wishing the delirium that had captured him earlier would return.

His mother bent over him, searching his eyes. "You can't deny it, Adam. Why can't I encourage her to overlook your shortcomings?"

"Overlook my…" He gave up.

Adam spotted his father's defeated gaze and swallowed his frustration. What would he do without them?

The next afternoon, Adam lay alone, his thoughts in turmoil. He knew he'd made a mistake admitting his feelings to Kate, and worse, letting his mother see it in his face.

Kate filled his every thought. Where had those amazing sensations come from? Maybe Kate was right. She had called him spoiled and said he enjoyed the personal attention, but he didn't think so. She'd meant more to him than that.

For one thing, she'd helped him focus on what was

important. In his moaning and groaning, he'd forgotten to lean on the Lord. He was trying to do that now but, he had to admit, his promise had grown worse instead of better.

A chill shuddered down his back, and he clamped his jaw closed to contain the sensation that swept over him. He was a physician. Adam recognized a problem, and he had one. He'd felt hot earlier; now ice ran through his veins.

He'd gotten one injection on top of another. But why? He still felt miserable. His mind wavered in a daze, and his chest felt paralyzed. If he had the strength, he would pound the walls to get someone to listen. He'd pushed the nurse call button earlier and no one had come. Change of shift, he'd figured. Adam knew he should be feeling better, not worse.

And Kate. She'd turned her back on him when he needed her. He trusted Kate's opinion. She knew her business. Kate was a top-notch nurse.

His body tingled and he struggled to remain conscious. Think. Focus. He willed himself to be alert. He needed help.

Please. Kate. I need you. Adam rolled his head against the pillow.

His sweet Kate. He clung to her image. He wanted her for more than her nursing skills. It had taken a tragedy to make him realize that Kate meant the world to him.

In the midst of his muddled thoughts, Adam saw a flicker at the doorway. He pulled himself from the haze and saw Kate watching him.

"Are you okay?"

"No. I'm not."

"If you need something, I'll tell your nurse. What is it?"

A numbing sensation rolled through his limbs and he grasped his chest, willing away the disturbing feeling. Perspiration beaded his forehead, yet he'd begun to tremble. "You've been avoiding me."

He tried to look at her but his vision blurred.

"I'm not avoiding you. I'm back to work. I have my own patient load. If you need something, I'll tell your nurse."

"I'm feeling very odd, Kate. Something's definitely wrong."

She raised her eyebrows and shook her head. "I'll get your nurse."

He studied her through the haze. "I'm not joking, Kate."

"Look, Adam, do you need some pain meds? Is that it?"

"I just had an injection…again. I'm having a bad reaction to something."

"Who's your nurse today?"

His attitude startled her. She thought he was vying for her attention. Today it was more than that. He enjoyed her fussing over him, but today something was seriously wrong.

She shrugged. "I'll get someone."

Defeat crushed him as he watched Kate turn away. Since he'd let her know how he felt—and then his mother's intervention—she'd pulled away. He wasn't imagining it. She'd changed. Not that she hadn't been attentive with him when he was her patient, but she wasn't his Kate.

The icy feeling rolled through him again. Adam

fumbled to draw the blanket around his neck, praying the unnerving sensation would pass. He tried to breathe. His lungs seemed empty. No air. The room spun. He felt light-headed.

Adam aimed his clouded eyes toward the door, praying Kate would return. Anyone. He attempted to organize his thoughts. Being a surgeon, he should be able to diagnose his illness by the symptoms. Something…but he couldn't think.

Instead of Kate, his mother came through the doorway in a blur. The only color that registered was the green in her volunteer's smock that wavered in and out of his vision. She gave him a little wave as she approached, then she faltered.

"Adam? You look terrible."

She hurried forward and pressed her palm against his face. "You're ice cold, and you're perspiring."

"I—I…I'm…I think they…gave m-me—" His words slurred and his mind failed him. His mother's panicked face wove in and out of focus.

"Gave you what?" She hovered over him, worry distorting her features. "You're deathly white. I'm frightened, Adam. I'll get a nurse." She stepped away.

"Get K-Kate," Adam whispered, forming the words in his mouth though his voice seemed to float above him.

Liza darted toward the doorway, the green cloth of her jacket appearing as dark billows ready to wash over him like a tidal wave. Colors faded to misty gray, and a buzz hummed in his ears. He gasped for a breath but his lungs seemed frozen.

He felt paralyzed.

"Dear Lord," he prayed, "help me."

Chapter Ten

Fiona's Stagecoach Café was busy on Monday afternoon when Sam steered Colleen to a corner table. Fiona gave them a cheerful wave and pranced to their table with the coffeepot.

"How are you, Colleen? It's been a long time since you've dropped in."

"I'm fine, Aunt Fiona." She motioned toward Sam. "You know Sam Vance."

"I sure do. He's one of my best customers."

"I keep coming back for that famous apple pie of yours," Sam said. He figured Fiona liked her pie, too, noting her rounded form like a figure eight. "Any left?"

Her brown eyes sparkled, and she flashed him a wink. "Always pie for you, Sam." She lifted the carafe. "Coffee?"

"Sure thing."

Fiona picked up his mug, then used her arm to

brush her bright red hair from her eyes while balancing the scalding hot coffee carafe above him.

Sam leaned away, waiting for a catastrophe, but none happened, and Fiona only laughed as she poured the brew.

"A waitress will be here in a minute. The special today is a smoked salmon Caesar salad." She eyed the kitchen door. "Now I'd better get back there and keep an eye on the help."

Sam watched as she made her way through the tables, greeting customers and topping off coffee, before he turned to Colleen.

"Thanks for meeting me," he said, unfolding the paper napkin and placing it on his lap.

Colleen grinned, her cropped blond hair spiked in unruly directions. "Happy to. Don't forget, you're buying me lunch."

"Guess I am."

She paused and gave him the once-over. "You're a good-looking man, Sam. If you weren't a friend of my brother's, I might make a play for you."

Sam didn't know how to respond to her flirtatious words, so he took a swig of coffee. He thought of Colleen as one of the Montgomery boys although he had to admit she was a woman. No doubt about it.

Before any more was said, the waitress arrived. "Ready?" she asked.

"Colleen?" Sam said, remembering to be polite. He ate with his partner so often, he could easily forget good etiquette.

"I'll have the salad…with grilled chicken." She turned up her nose. "I don't like salmon," she whispered.

Sam waited while the woman jotted down the order, until she looked at him. "Roasted pork green chili."

"That's it?" the woman asked.

"And coffee," he said, motioning to his cup.

She scribbled it on her pad and left.

Sam turned and eyed the folder Colleen had placed on the corner of the table. "So what do you have for me?"

"Not sure this will help, but I got a good story out of it. My editor's pleased. Anytime you have a story line, don't be afraid to suggest it."

Delaying her answer bugged him. Sam wanted facts. "Tell me what you're hoarding in that file." He pointed a finger at the manila folder.

Colleen grinned and flipped it open. "Here's what I think you want."

She handed him the sheet of notes, and he scanned the information, his pulse throbbing like a police siren. Names, nicknames, drugs references and possible drug-buy locations. He eyed her over the paper. "How did you get all this?"

"It wasn't easy, but when women are abused and frustrated, some are willing to talk. They're tired of their lives, but afraid to say too much. Like you said, they would never talk with the police, but I was a reporter who promised to not use names...and I'm a woman. They trust me."

"I didn't think you'd get this much," Sam said, regarding the volume of information she had provided.

She tapped the manila folder. "Desperation creates brilliance. Women fighting for their lives listen. They nose around. Telephone conversations. Scribbled notes left behind. They'd rather learn it's drugs than another woman. Sad, but in this case, informative.'' She tossed her head showing her confidence.

Sam gave the paper a whack with the back of his hand. "You did great." The information arranged itself in his mind. With it, he might obtain cooperation from one of the men involved in the saloon fight. The department could make some real progress then. The witness was still in the hospital and not happy to be there. Once Sam let him know they had names and places, he may spit out what he'd refused to tell earlier.

Colleen leaned back, eyeing him. "Glad I could help."

Sam folded the paper and slipped it into his pocket.

Colleen took a sip from her glass and leaned closer. "By the way, did you notice the reference to Vance Memorial in my notes?" She motioned toward his pocket.

"Vance Memorial?" He felt a frown settle on his face and reached in and withdrew the paper. He scanned the contents. *Vance Memorial.* His pulse skipped at the notation.

"Surprised?" Colleen asked. "I was."

"Shocked is more like it." He read the reference again. Three women had made notes hearing, "Vance Memorial," in telephone conversations between husbands and drug dealers.

"What do you think? Is someone slipping drugs out of the hospital?"

Sam's mind zinged with prospects. If it were true, it put a whole new spin on the situation in Venezuela.

"I'm not sure." But it was something he'd investigate. He could check with Records and talk with the burglary division. He rubbed his chin while his brain shot out possibilities.

Colleen's voice broke into his thoughts. "Or the theft might have been kept in house... You know, someone was afraid to let the world know that Vance Memorial got careless with their drugs."

Sam had considered that, too. "Could be. Then again, maybe it's nothing."

Colleen shrugged. "Anyway, do what you will with it. I hope it helps."

Sam refolded the paper and tucked it back into his pocket.

The waitress came and slid their orders onto the table and slipped away, promising to return with more coffee.

While his thoughts whirled, Sam took a spoonful of chili, then scanned the café crowd. His gaze came to a dead halt when he spotted Alistair Barclay seated in a back booth. As always, the hotel mogul was accompanied by a well-dressed woman, too plastered with makeup for an afternoon luncheon. Sam caught the twinkle of a handful of diamonds—or cubic zirconia—but he'd never know the difference.

The woman's crossed legs toyed with Barclay's beneath the table and the man chucked her under the chin, then brushed his hand over his reddish plastered-down comb-over.

Something about him grated Sam's nerves. Maybe his overdone British accent or his gray eyes that peered below bushy brows. Whatever, Sam felt wary of the man who'd walked into Colorado Springs three years earlier and started buying up prime property at top dollar and putting up luxury hotels. Sam despised what he'd done to the Montgomerys. He almost sensed a personal vendetta, but that didn't make sense.

"What's wrong?" Colleen asked, glancing over her shoulder.

"Alistair Barclay is with another one of his flashy ladies over there."

He tilted his head in their direction and Colleen let her gaze drift toward his nod.

She looked at Sam and rolled her eyes. "I don't know the man, but I've heard enough about him. I hate what he's doing to our family. From what Dad says, he's sure stealing the business away from Montgomery Construction."

"I know. I wish he'd take his playboy antics and move to some other town. We don't need his kind here. He should head back to Britain where he belongs."

"Sorry to disillusion you, Sam. I remember when the *Sentinel* made a big deal out of Barclay getting his U.S. citizenship. He's not likely to head back to England now."

The food stuck in Sam's chest like a wad of clay and he was sorry he'd let himself get riled over Barclay. Between Barclay and the information in his pocket, the day had turned dark.

Kate raced into the hospital room with Liza on her heels. As soon as she saw Adam again, she knew he was in trouble. Without delay, she rammed the call button. She heard the static from the nurses' station.

"A physician. Stat." Her voice pierced the air.

Tears welled in her eyes. Adam could be dying. But why? What had happened?

"Breathe, Adam," she called. "Take a deep breath."

She fought to remain calm, not wanting to frighten Adam's mother, who hovered beside her.

"He'll be fine," Kate said, to reassure Liza. "Once the doctor arrives, he'll be okay."

Heavenly Father, Kate cried out in silence, *be with him. Save him.*

Liza sank into the chair beside her son and clung to his hand. "Do as Kate says, Adam. Take a deep breath."

Footsteps pounded in the corridor, and Kate stepped aside as Dr. Fletcher and his team raced through the doorway.

"Clear the room, ladies," he ordered.

Liza bounded from the chair and bumped into Kate as they backed toward the exit. Kate watched Robert Fletcher grab his chart and flip to the last page. He scanned the sheet, concern charging across his face. The chart tumbled to the floor.

"Naloxone. Stat."

Naloxone. Kate heard the word. An antidote for a narcotics overdose. Fear glued her to the floor. Her heart thundered, imagining the possibilities. Adam's respiration would slow and stop unless...

Guilt and fear overwhelmed her. If she'd been his nurse, nothing would have happened. How did he overdose? Who could have made such a horrible error?

Kate pulled herself together for Liza's sake. "Let's

go to the nurses' station and wait there. They need space to work.'' She curved her arm around the woman's shoulders and steered her away from the dire scene. Though Kate's feet led her down the hallway, her heart stayed with Adam.

Once Liza had settled onto a chair with a cup of tea, Kate ventured back toward Adam's room. The team still worked over him, but Kate saw his hand move, and her heart lifted. He was alive. For now.

Freed from hiding her emotions, Kate allowed tears to roll down her cheeks. She brushed them away with her fingers and captured enough courage to go through the doorway. ''Is he—''

Robert Fletcher nodded. ''You saved his life... again, Kate. He's coming around.''

She buried her face in her hands and wept while her prayer of thanksgiving soared to heaven. But questions still rocked her sense of relief. What had happened and why? Then another question struck her. Who?

As she turned to go, Robert Fletcher called her name and she turned back.

''I want to talk with you in a minute.''

Kate pointed down the hallway. ''I'll be at the nurses' station.'' She left and hurried down the hallway, eyeing her patients' rooms and making sure another nurse had taken over for her. She'd been so grateful when a new colleague had seen her distress and offered to help.

Liza was standing by the doorway when she returned. ''How is he?'' Her pale face was blotched with fear.

"Dr. Fletcher said he's coming around. I think he'll be okay."

"What happened?" Liza asked.

Kate swallowed her confusion. "I don't know. The doctor will be here in a minute. Maybe he can tell us."

Pulling herself together, Kate returned to her patients and carried on her duties until the doctor beckoned to her from a doorway to follow him. Instead of returning to the nurses' station, he took her into the floor kitchen next door.

"Kate, I don't want Adam's mother to hear this right now."

She felt her stomach recoil at his words. "What is it?"

"As you know, Adam had a narcotic overdose. I need to talk to the nurse who cared for him today. Look at his chart."

Kate took the clipboard from Robert Fletcher's hand and scanned the information. "He's had two powerful injections in less than an hour. Who would do this?"

The doctor shook his head. "Who is his nurse?"

"Grace Roth. She's worked here for years. I can't believe she'd make a mistake."

"I need to talk with her. Would you ask her to come in?"

Kate's pulse raced as she left to find Grace.

When she located Grace, the woman's face paled, but she followed Kate to where Robert Fletcher was waiting.

Kate left them alone and checked in with the nurse

handling her patients, then hurried back to Adam's room.

Liza was already there, sitting beside her son, her hand covering his. Adam slept while one of Kate's colleagues worked nearby checking his IV. Kate stood in the doorway until she finished, then came into the room.

Liza looked at her with tear-filled eyes. "This is almost more than I can bear. I've asked the Lord to keep him safe, but—"

"You have to trust God. I know it's difficult and we don't always understand His purpose."

Liza nodded. "I know. It's just…" She lowered her head, letting the sobs flow freely.

Kate gave in to her own grief. "I can't imagine how this will serve anything good, but we only see through blinded eyes. One day we'll understand."

But Kate wanted to understand *today*. She bent over Liza and pressed her cheek against the woman's graying hair. Her usual rosy cheeks had paled, and anger swelled inside Kate. She agreed. Why would the Lord let this happen? What nurse had made such a horrible mistake?

Her anger turned to guilt. If she'd been there for Adam…if she'd insisted on being his nurse, she would have caught the error before it happened. Who? Why? How? The questions burned in her mind.

"He'll be fine tomorrow," she said, convincing herself as well as Liza. "He needs to sleep off the narcotics, and when he wakes he'll be his old self."

"I don't understand," Liza whispered, her face pressed against her arm. Her voice was muted by her sleeve.

Kate didn't understand, either, and she struggled with the decision to stay with Adam and Liza or go to find Robert Fletcher.

Her decision ended when the doctor appeared in the doorway. "There you are."

She stepped toward him. "I was checking on Adam. He'll be okay." She wasn't sure if her words were a statement or a question.

"I'm confident he'll pull through this. You caught it in time. Otherwise..." His voice faded as he flagged her to his side and drew her outside. "We have a serious problem, Kate."

His grave look numbed her. "I know, but...what did Grace say?"

"Grace knew nothing about this."

Bewildered, Kate couldn't respond.

"This wasn't an accident."

Kate's hand flew to her heart to hold back its thudding. "What do you mean?"

"A doctor called the nurses' desk and said to give Adam an additional 2 cc's of Demerol directly into his IV. Grace was off the floor, so the nurse on duty followed the doctor's orders."

Kate's mind whirred with confusion. "Who? What doctor would do that?"

"The nurse said Dr. Fletcher had called in the order."

"Dr. Fletcher? You?" Kate's legs trembled and she fell against the wall to brace herself.

"It wasn't me, Kate. Someone used my name. She's new and didn't know my voice."

"Another doctor?"

''Not necessarily. It could be anyone with a knowledge of medicine.''

She searched his face, hoping he had an explanation for the mix-up. His expression seemed as dire and shocked as she felt.

''I talked to the hospital director. He's notifying the police.''

''Police? What does this mean?'' Kate covered her face with her hands, already knowing the answer to the question.

Someone had tried to kill Adam.

Chapter Eleven

After a sleepless morning, Kate hurried along the corridor and came to a halt before she reached Adam's door. A police officer sat outside. The reality smacked her in the solar plexus. Her memory reeled with the reality from yesterday. Someone wanted to harm Adam.

What had he done to trigger such hatred? Was the murder attempt connected with the crime in Venezuela? It all seemed too far-fetched, but Kate could find no other answers.

She nodded at the young officer and walked through the doorway. Her shift didn't start until evening, but she had come back early, too riled by the incident to rest.

The privacy curtain was drawn, but she saw feet move below it and knew someone was inside. She pushed past the cloth, her mind conjuring more problems…more evil. Instead, she faced Dr. Fletcher. His quick look let her know he felt on edge, as well.

"How is he?" Kate asked, moving toward the bed.

"He's still sleeping and probably will most of the day. It's not a coma, but we need to keep an eye on him." He gestured toward the IV bag hanging from a pole. "I have him on glucose and thiamine now, and we're continuing a small dose of Naloxone."

"Any complications?" Kate's chest tightened, waiting for the physician's response.

"No results yet from the blood tests. Hopefully not, but you never know with an overdose. Naturally we need to watch the liver and kidneys." Robert Fletcher checked his pulse, then listened to Adam's heart.

She nodded, knowing those organs were at the highest risk.

"I'll order an EKG, too," the doctor said, adjusting the IV drip.

Kate pulled her fingers through her hair and leaned against the bed rail. "I don't understand. Why Adam? I didn't think he had any enemies."

He shrugged. "Must be some nut. Why do people do any of the crazy things they do?"

Kate sank into a nearby chair. "I see the police have a guard in the corridor."

He nodded. "Sad, isn't it? We had the police swarming here all last night. You saw them."

"I left early, but I did see them. I couldn't take it. I couldn't concentrate."

"I know it's difficult. We'll all feel better when we find out who did this…or how it happened." He turned to face her. "I'm afraid to even speculate."

Kate massaged her face. Her head ached, her eyes burned.

Robert Fletcher moved toward the doorway. "Are you working?"

"Not today, but I'm on tonight. Right now I'm just keeping an eye on him. Tomorrow's my day off."

"Good. You need some rest, too."

"I know I need a break…but I'm sure I'll hang around the hospital anyway."

She saw the stress in Robert Fletcher's face. "I'm glad you're here, Kate. Keep an eye on him. Try to rouse him if you can. We don't want him slipping into a coma."

"I'll be right here."

He slid past the curtain while Kate rose and moved the chair closer to Adam's bed.

She leaned her head back, her mind rutted in sorrow and frustration. How could evil have penetrated her world so deeply? Venezuela. Here at home, where she should feel safe. Vance Memorial, where doctors and nurses saved lives. A place of safety turned into a place of peril. How much longer would it last?

She focused on Adam. She'd always admired his handsome face, the classic line of his jaw and his full mouth. Once again, he seemed so lifeless…empty. Her heart broke with the vision.

"Adam." She gave his arm a nudge.

His head moved a fraction.

"Let's talk. We have to think this thing through. Who's out to do evil…and why?"

His eyes remained closed.

But she would persist. She wouldn't allow him to slip into a coma. The world needed his talent.

And Kate needed…a friend.

* * *

Adam awakened feeling as if he'd been on a two-week drinking binge…and he didn't drink. His mouth felt like cotton, and the room spun when he lifted his head for water. He looked toward his door and saw it was closed. He wasn't sure what day it was…or what had happened.

He dropped his head against the pillow and hit the nurse's call button. The last he remembered was feeling peculiar. Nothing after that…except a vague recollection of his mother wearing something green that seemed like waves rolling toward him.

"Yes?" the voice said.

"Ish…" He tried to work his mouth again. "Ish K-Kate…?" He gave up. His words slipped around without control, like marbles on ice.

He watched the doorway, hoping Kate would hear his plea and come to his rescue. Why did he feel so rotten?

Adam tried to focus on the wall calendar, but the numbers and letters blurred, melting into alien shapes. He concentrated. July 16? He forced his head forward. Yes. Sixteen. A Friday. He twisted toward the window. Daylight. He barely remembered yesterday. He'd been so ill.

Footsteps pulled his attention to the doorway. His anticipation rose, but when the figure came through, his heart sank.

"Adam, we need to talk," Sam said.

"Whass hap-pened? Ish…" He shifted his tongue, then gave up.

"You had an overdose of narcotics."

The words flitted through Adam's head. Had he heard Sam correctly? "Overdose?"

"Demerol, I think."

Adam motioned toward the water carafe.

Sam sloshed some liquid into a paper cup and handed it to him with a straw. "Dry?"

He nodded as he drew in the soothing moisture. "When did thish hap-pen?"

Sam grinned. "Sounds like you've had one too many." His face grew serious. "And I guess you did. A couple of cc's too many."

"But how?"

Sam squirmed and looked away.

Adam tried to raise himself, but the room spiraled and he sank against the mattress. "Jush tell me."

"Someone wanted to kill you."

The sentence bounced into his mind one word at a time, and Adam struggled to connect the thought and line up each word in a neat mental row. Kill him? He steered his gaze toward Sam. Was he kidding?

Sam's serious expression answered his question.

Adam rubbed his hand over his face, wanting to feel alive, but he didn't. When he lifted his arm to gesture, he noticed the IV. Would it ever end?

The door opened again, and Kate came through, bringing sunshine into Adam's dreary day. Kate would explain. She would tell him it was all a mistake…or a poor joke.

Her gaze drifted to Sam, then to Adam. "How are you?"

"Don't ashk."

Concern rose beneath her faint smile. "You look rotten." She motioned to the doorway. "I see there's still an officer outside."

"It's his cousin," Sam said.

Adam pushed his fingers against his eyes. "Brendan—Uncle Joe and Aunt Fiona's son?"

"Yes. We're not taking any more chances," Sam said. "Someone will be out there as long as it takes."

Kate dropped her shoulder bag on the end of the bed. "You're here bright and early."

"Adam and I have some business," he said.

"Do you think he can even think right now?"

Adam enjoyed seeing her protectiveness. A nurse's prerogative, but he wondered if it were more than that.

Sam shook his head. "Sorry. Time is of the essence. The investigation needs Adam's input."

"I thought you weren't on the case," Kate said as she sat on the edge of Adam's bed.

"I am now."

"If I have to think, would you help me up?" Adam asked, motioning to Kate.

She rose and pulled away the blankets, then helped him to shift his weight forward.

He inched his legs over the edge, and Kate put her arm around his shoulder and helped him sit.

"Thanks," Adam said. "I'm really woozy."

"That's to be expected." Sam pulled a small notebook from his pocket and a pen. "You can both help me."

Kate settled beside Adam again. He could smell the scent of her shampoo, citrus and herbs…and a sweetness that pulled at his heartstrings. Perfume, he thought. Something exotic. The aroma took him back to Venezuela, and he saw Kate again in the shadow of the chinaberry tree, the sun spreading its colors against her hair.

"Adam?"

Adam jolted from his reverie.

Sam gave him an odd look, then posed his pen. "Tell me again who was at the clinic with you in Santa Maria de Flores. I know Valenti was there."

Kate shifted beside him. "Dr. Gordon Reese, surgeon. Dr. Dan Eckerd. He's in pediatrics. Dr. Rana Sahir. She's in cardiology."

"Did the last two doctors come back with you?" he asked Kate.

"Not on the plane with us. The next day, I think."

Sam took notes. "Is that it?"

Adam felt himself sway as exhaustion rolled over him. "Technicians. Lab. X-ray." He realized his speech had improved.

"And we had three doctors from another Colorado Springs hospital," Kate said.

"Names?"

Kate rattled off the names. "But you don't think anyone we know—"

Sam's gaze pinned her. "We check every lead." He shifted his coat lapel to put away the pen, then paused. "The other day you mentioned a woman that worked with you at the clinic."

"Carmen Clemente. She lives in Santa Maria de Flores. She cleaned and did odd jobs, translated when we got stumped."

He jotted her name into the notebook. "I wonder if she has connections here."

"Connections?" Adam was thrown by the comment.

"The Diablo Syndicate."

"A crime syndicate?" Kate asked.

"Why couldn't it have a connection with Venezuela? Diablo sounds Spanish to me," Sam said.

Kate frowned. "It's Spanish, but that's a little far-fetched."

"Maybe. Maybe not," Sam said.

"What else do you need from me?" Adam asked.

Kate did a double take. "You're not slurring your words, Adam."

"My head's not spinning as much."

"So much is up in the air, Adam. We need you to remember. Are you prodding yourself? Are you trying? We really need—"

"Don't you think I want to remember as much as you want me to, Sam?" Adam massaged his jaw with his hands, his face riddled with frustration.

"I'm sorry. We're all frustrated. I'm sure you are, too."

"I understand. It's…" Adam shook his head and stopped as if he had nothing more to add.

Sam rose. "Listen, I'll let you rest, but I'll tell you what else I really need to know." He turned to Kate. "You were the one who got to Adam first in Venezuela. I need to go over details. Sound by sound. Movement by movement. There might be something we're missing that'll help us."

"When do you want to talk?" she asked.

"How about now? We could go for a coffee and let Adam rest."

"Now's not good. I have a meeting at the Galilee Women's Shelter."

"Lunch tomorrow? How about the Stagecoach Café? Adam's aunt Fiona owns the place."

Kate grinned. "The famous apple pie?"

"You got it." Sam slid his hand in his pocket and stepped toward the door. "What's going on at the shelter?"

"I'm helping with a fund-raiser with Adam's mother. It's some kind of auction."

"Art?" Adam asked.

Kate shrugged. "I don't know the details."

Sam slipped off his jacket and tossed it over his shoulder. "Probably one of those white elephant things. People auctioning off their junk."

"One person's junk is another person's treasure," Kate said.

"That's true enough." Sam raised his hand. "See you tomorrow at noon."

Kate stood and watched him go. If he weren't so abrupt and all about the case, he'd be a hunk. Still, Kate sensed he had Adam's good at heart and a job to do.

"What did you think of Sam?" Adam asked.

"He's okay, but I don't like that he bugs you."

"I'd think a good-looking stallion like that would sway you to get out your lasso." He touched her arm, then urged her to sit beside him.

"I can't deny he's handsome, but then…" She let her gaze travel over Adam's drawn, tired face. "If we're talking horses, I prefer an Arabian myself—intelligent, well-bred. No need to rope and tie them."

Adam gave her a puzzled smile. "Did you have one in mind?" He slid his hand along her arm and rested his palm on her hand.

Kate clutched the sheet, afraid to enjoy the intimate

pleasure that wove through her chest. "I'm looking," she said, hoping he didn't hear how breathless she was.

"You're tense," Adam said, shifting his hand to squeeze her shoulder.

"It's all the questions…all the problems since this horrible ordeal happened." She shifted to face him. "And now, this thing with you." She gestured toward the IV. "You feel it, too."

His fingers worked along the cords of her neck and Kate relaxed with his touch.

His hands faltered. "Sure, I feel it. I'm tired of the questions. I'm frustrated because I can't remember a thing, and…"

Adam's voice trailed off while Kate waited, hoping he'd state what was on his mind. He needed to talk, and she was anxious to listen.

Finally he dropped his hands and gave her a direct look. "I'm scared silly. Someone wants me dead. I have no idea what's going on. For the first time in my life, I feel helpless. Out of control. Frightened."

She took his hand in hers and held it in her lap. She felt his blood pulsate through his body…his cold hands—skilled, wonderful hands—had grown weak from all the recent traumatic events.

"I'm defenseless, Kate. I've paraded around my whole life looking self-assured. Confident." He sent her a wry smile. "Even a little cocky."

She gave him an eager nod, hoping to release the stress that wracked them both.

"I've been a believer and tried to do what God wants me to do. I've given to others—time, talent, treasures."

He slipped his hand beneath hers, cupping it in both of his while his eyes pleaded. "But this is the first time in my life I feel helpless and know I need God's mercy and protection."

"And love," Kate said.

He turned to her with questioning eyes.

"We all need to understand that God loves His children. I've watched your father strut and fret since you've been in here. He pounds his fists and bellows about lawsuits and negligence."

Adam's expression softened with the hint of a grin. "That's my dad."

"And he does it for you, Adam. Why? Because he loves you so much. Our heavenly Father's love is even greater than that."

Adam didn't speak, but Kate could sense he understood what she was saying.

"'But the Lord is faithful,'" she continued, "'and he will strengthen and protect you from the evil one.' It's in Thessalonians. It's a favorite verse of mine, because it shows us the depth of God's love and power."

Their own silence surrounded them. Footsteps clicked in the hallway. Voices drifted along the corridor. The overhead light gave a faint hum, but they said nothing.

"Thank you," Adam said finally. He reached over and caressed her cheek.

The gentle touch raced through her, weaving into her emotions and stirring her longing.

Surprised, Kate looked into his eyes and was startled by the mist she saw there. She opened her arms, and Adam closed the distance between them, resting his head against her head. His body pressed against her shoulder and her heart thundered at his nearness.

Why am I doing this, Lord? The question rocked her serenity.

Adam wasn't the only one who'd become vulnerable. He wasn't the only one taking chances. Kate could only reap hurt and sadness once Adam was well and out of the hospital. He had never liked her. Yet here she'd stayed, like that little lapdog. The wagging-tail puppy willing to lick the crumbs from the floor. Still, she couldn't stop herself. Right now, they needed each other.

"Could we pray together?" she asked, releasing her grip and easing back.

He eyed her with a puzzled look.

She didn't ask its meaning.

Adam nodded, and they joined hands.

Kate kept her voice modulated, slow and steady, hoping Adam wouldn't sense her wavering emotions. "Heavenly Father, we are Your children and need Your loving care. Hold Your hand over us and protect us from evil. Give us strength and comfort in this time of terror."

She felt Adam's hand grip hers and sensed the internal struggle he dealt with to pray aloud. "And, Lord, I thank You for keeping me here on earth a little longer. Let me feel Your presence in my life. In Jesus' name."

Their amens joined as one.

Hearing his prayer, Kate's heart veered off course. She was losing the battle with reality. Her heart was winning.

Chapter Twelve

Kate's mind lingered on her talk with Sam as she pulled into the Galilee Women's Shelter parking lot and climbed out of Adam's car. She eyed the facility, a three-story sandstone structure with a broad front porch that ran its length. She felt saddened that the impressive building was located in the least respected part of town.

As she drew closer, she witnessed the contrast of the newer redbrick two-story building that appeared to connect two older sections. With so many doors, she didn't know where to enter. She assumed walking into the women's shelter would be inappropriate. They valued their privacy.

"Kate."

She swung around and saw Liza waving to her from the parking lot. Kate waited, pleased Adam's mother had arrived to solve her quandary.

"The redbrick addition houses the administrative offices," Liza said. She waved her forward, and Kate went ahead, holding the door open for the petite woman.

"I hope this meeting didn't throw you off schedule," Liza said. "I know you have so much to do."

"No, it's fine. I need a diversion from all the stress."

"You poor dear. It's all so frightening, isn't it? I can't believe someone wants to harm Adam. I haven't slept well since it happened."

"Same for me," Kate said. "It's too hard to believe."

Their heels tapped along the empty corridor, and when they reached the conference room, Liza led the way inside and greeted a woman standing at the long table.

Jessica Mathers lifted her head and gave Kate a friendly smile. Her light brown hair rounded into a soft cap framing her pleasant face. Her manner struck Kate as a woman who knew her business and had the drive to make things happen. But it wasn't only her professional qualities that really caught Kate's attention. Kate connected immediately with the look in Jessica's gray eyes. Something deeper—past hurts or present longings—some fragile aura that roused Kate's curiosity.

"Welcome," Jessica said, moving toward Kate with her arm extended.

"Thank you," Kate said, accepting her slender hand. "I'm glad I can help."

"Liza has told me so much about you. You're rather a heroine, I understand."

Kate shook her head. "Not really. God just put me in the right place at the right time."

"I'm sure everyone's thankful," Jessica said. She motioned to the chairs around the table. "Have a seat. We're waiting on a couple more ladies, and then our shelter director wants to stop in and say hello."

Kate pulled out a chair situated closest to the door and sat. Though pleased to support the program, being there left her uneasy, knowing she had so little to offer and feeling too familiar with the horrific stories that surrounded the women making their home at the shelter.

Liza joined her, then greeted two other women who arrived and made introductions. They seemed genial and conversation centered on the community and their private lives.

In a few minutes, an exquisite-looking woman with sparkling dark eyes and short black hair that fell in corkscrew curls just below her ears stepped through the doorway. Her broad smile—enhanced by white teeth contrasting her mahogany skin—brightened the room.

"So good to have you here," she said. "I'm Susan Carter, director of Galilee Women's Shelter. I've met a couple of you before, but again, I want to welcome you to the shelter and thank you from the bottom of my heart for your willingness to do Jesus' work for those who have such great needs."

The group murmured their responses, flattered yet humble because they knew serving was one of God's commandments.

"Our work would be much more difficult without the help of Jessica Mathers who handles all our fund-raising and contributions. Jessica is fairly new to us, but her understanding of the need and her true devotion to the cause has made a huge difference since she's been with us. I want to thank her from the bottom of my heart.''

Quiet applause rippled around the room while Jessica lifted her hand to graciously silence them.

Susan took a step backward. "I'll let you get on with your work, but again, welcome and thank you so much for your willingness to volunteer.''

As Susan left the room, Jessica rose from her place at the table and passed around a handout. "Our purpose today is to look at the jobs that need to be done and see where you feel you can best fit in. Take a look at the list and see which task might work for you and your schedule.'' She paused a moment. "Does anyone have a preference?''

"I usually work nights,'' Kate said, "so I'd be happy to make some follow-up calls for donations. I'm not sure I'll have evenings available for the other jobs.''

"No problem.'' She looked at the women, studying the paper. "Anyone else?''

Kate eyed the sheet again. "I'll stuff invitation envelopes, too.'' Anything to fill her time with something other than mooning over Adam. It would also help her keep her thoughts from the awful things that had happened since the shooting.

"We need lots of stuffers,'' Jessica said, sending her a teasing smile. "Others?''

Liza volunteered to join Kate in stuffing envelopes. Others jumped in to take on other tasks.

Kate marveled at their eagerness. The shelter had stirred thoughts of her childhood—days when she and her mother had no food to eat and nights with no bed to sleep in. She gazed around the room at the enthusiastic faces filled with concern for others.

And Jessica. Kate saw compassion and generosity in the woman's thoughtful eyes. What sorrow did she still harbor? Kate hid her own problems so well, she had learned to spot them in others.

As the discussion proceeded, Kate's curiosity grew. "I'm volunteering to help, and I have no idea what this fund-raiser is."

Jessica's eyes widened. "Good question. I thought everyone knew. This is one of this year's larger efforts. It's unique and I think will be a lot of fun...and get a lot of press."

Liza gave a little laugh and aroused Kate's curiosity.

"We're having a silent auction with a starting bid of one thousand dollars. Some single men of our community have agreed to be auctioned off along with a dream date package."

Dream dates? Kate couldn't imagine.

Within seconds, Jessica answered her unspoken question. "Some dates will include activities such as a romantic dinner party at the Broadmoor, a golf weekend, a whitewater rafting adventure, three days at the Lost Valley Ranch, a spa weekend, season tickets to a sports venue. We've been soliciting some wonderful prizes."

"Sounds intriguing," Kate said. "What a great idea." An unbidden vision rose in her head of her and Adam enjoying a romantic dinner at the Broadmoor or enjoying a whitewater adventure. "How did you coerce the bachelors?"

Jessica folded her hands across her chest. "Our single men didn't have a chance when their mothers and grandmothers came to our aid. I'm sure we have a few reluctant men, but they're all being good sports.''

"My own son volunteered," Liza said.

Kate's enthusiasm sank. Adam? Would he have agreed to be raffled off? She studied Liza's face, afraid to ask. And if he did, Kate didn't have a thousand dollars to even make the opening bid.

"Jake's a good sport," Jessica said, halting Kate's concern. "I was pleased he agreed."

Kate's shoulders relaxed. The ambiguous feelings confused her. Adam had caressed her cheek and held her hand, but Kate faced facts. She was a diversion. He was recovering from an injury and complications. He was only amusing himself until he was well. That was it. How often had he said he wanted his freedom? Being tied to a relationship certainly took a bite out of independence.

Throughout her life, Kate had experienced plenty of freedom. More than she'd bargained for…more than she could bear. Walking hand in hand with someone might feel wonderful. Her hand warmed envisioning Adam's fingers embracing hers.

"What do you think of our project, Kate?" Jessica asked. "What brings you here besides Liza's prodding?"

Kate grinned at Adam's mother. For a gentle woman, she did pack a wallop when it came to evoking action.

"I'm a nurse," Kate said. "I've worked with a lot of needy, hurting people. I just returned from Venezuela where my heart broke for the families so embedded in poverty that their lives seemed hopeless.

My goal is to help people. I try to keep their hopes alive. I know that bad things happen to good people—'' Kate felt her throat constrict, thinking back to her own personal struggles ''—and I'd like to be part of giving them hope and help.''

"That's a wonderful, heartfelt mission," Jessica said.

Kate winced inside that she'd allowed herself to be so obvious. "Nurses see a lot of unfortunate things." She hoped her response camouflaged the truth.

Liza slid her hand across the tabletop and rested it on Kate's. She gave a comforting pat. Had Adam's mother read more into her comment than she'd wanted to reveal?

The dark shadows in Jessica's eyes made Kate wonder if their lives had followed a similar path. Kate sensed Jessica could be a good friend. She could talk with her and share her past…but not with Liza. She was wonderful, but she was Adam's mother. She would never truly accept Kate if she knew the truth.

And Adam could never know the details of her past. He would pity her, and she wanted no one's pity. She had pulled herself up from the depths and now had a career and an acceptable income. That's all she could ask for…and that's all she expected the good Lord to give her. He'd blessed her fully.

Unexpected, Liza's words rose in her thoughts. History and contribution don't make the person. God is what's important. "Rich and poor have this in common: The Lord is the Maker of them all."

The thought rolled over Kate. Could she be wrong? Would Liza accept her if she knew the truth?

* * *

Saturday afternoon, Sam turned on the car's air conditioner full blast. The temperature had risen and so had his anxiety. The case he'd been on seemed to head in so many directions. He hated ignoring Adam's questions but he couldn't talk about the case. He'd learned the victim in Venezuela had a connection with La Mano Oscura—the Dark Hand—a drug cartel. They hadn't nabbed the other perp. He was running free. But now, the question pressed on Sam's mind what a drug cartel would be doing in a clinic dispensary. He could only guess someone agreed to steal from the dispensary to pay off a local pusher who'd planned to sell the drugs on the black market.

Sam had also nosed around and finally hit pay dirt here at home. He'd learned that drugs, mainly narcotics, were heisted from Vance Memorial over a year ago. The drug issue seemed to be the main constant between Colorado Springs and Doctors Without Borders, but without more concrete information nothing made sense yet…but it would. He'd see to that.

When he pulled up to a stoplight, Sam glanced at his watch. He had a few minutes. He'd promised to meet Kate at the Stagecoach Café at noon. His mind struggled with her, too. What was her role in all this? Her relationship with Adam had all the makings of a romance, but they both appeared to be oblivious to it. Or was she?

With his eye for judging people, Sam couldn't imagine her being a part of the problems in Venezuela, but he couldn't be too careful. He'd tried to make sense out of it all, but neither Adam or Kate gave an inch. They were as closemouthed as he was.

His gaze drifted to the shade trees in Acacia Park on his right. The sun shimmered off his car hood. He'd give a five spot for a little less glare. He reached across the seat for his sunglasses. Leaning forward, he caught a glimpse of a silver Mercedes pulled to the side of the road. His father owned a silver Mercedes and his curiosity bumped a notch.

He rolled forward a car length, and his heart walloped against his chest. His father leaned against his car, his keys dangling from his fingers while Alistair Barclay stood beside him. Their conversation looked intense.

Sam's mind spun with concern. What would his father be doing talking to Barclay? Though the mogul had done nothing illegitimate that anyone could prove, the entire department had their eye on him. But mouths were shut and Sam didn't know why.

The light turned and Sam pulled away. He felt sick with apprehension. Max Vance's name was respected. Would he jeopardize it by getting involved with Barclay? Another jolt of worry jarred Sam's thoughts. His father had retired from the CIA a few years earlier. Had he been called back into service? Sam's heart slid to his feet. Not this close to home. No. Dad wouldn't endanger his family's lives.

Another idea shot through Sam's thoughts. Was his dad trying to get the goods on Barclay? He'd played havoc with the Montgomery family's construction company. Max had been bitter hearing how jobs had been stolen out from under them. Would he do that for an old friend?

Worse yet, was he probing without legal sanction?

He could jeopardize any investigation that might be ongoing and still put the Vances in danger.

Sam despised every possibility. His father was a well-respected citizen of Colorado Springs. He loved his family. Would he put either in jeopardy?

When it came down to seeing justice done, Sam had no idea.

Kate walked into the Stagecoach Café. She scanned the crowd and saw Sam beckoning her from a table in the rear. On her way, she noticed a buxom woman with the brightest red hair Kate had ever seen. Dyed, she thought. The manner in which she greeted guests and fluttered amid the tables made Kate suspect she was Aunt Fiona.

"Hi," Kate said when she reached Sam. "Sorry I'm a little late. I overslept…and I wanted to stop and check on Adam before coming here."

"How is he?"

Sam looked stressed, and Kate knew better than to ask.

"Doing better. He's still weak. This has been very trying for all of us. I'm weary myself."

He tilted back in his chair and folded his arms across his chest. "I'm curious. Why are you at his side day after day? Because you're a devoted colleague?" His look scrutinized her. "Is that the only reason?"

She arched a brow. "What questions did you have…besides that one?"

Sam didn't smile. He ignored her comment and handed her the menu. "Want to order first?"

She accepted it and scanned the fare, curious what

was bugging him. "I'll have the buffalo burger and a side salad."

He beckoned the waitress, placed their orders, then pulled his small spiral notebook and pen from his pocket. "I want you to describe the day for me, the day of the shooting. Try to think of anything unusual. Every detail might be important."

"What does this have to do with Adam's case?" Kate said.

"We have to check every angle, Kate. Things are happening. They seem connected or it's an amazing coincidence. That's all I can tell you."

Kate let the troubling information settle in her mind. "I don't believe in coincidence. I believe that God has a purpose and plan for us. We can fight the Lord's will, but if he wants it so, it happens. No coincidence."

"I agree. Anyway, I'm too suspicious to accept coincidence."

"You're a Christian?"

"Sure am." He put on his get-down-to-business face. "But we don't have time to discuss how a flat-foot sometimes puts his faith on the line. We need to talk about that day in Venezuela. The entire day."

"I wasn't questioning the faith issue," Kate said as she willed her mind to go back to that day…the full day. The vision lay muddied in her memory. "I feel the way Adam must feel. My mind seems to have blocked out what happened before the shooting."

"Please try to remember."

She sat a moment to gather her thoughts…to dredge up the day she wanted to forget. "The late shift began about six. Sometimes the evenings dragged. Other times they didn't. That day everyone seemed edgy. I remember we had a few patients that evening. One appointment I recall was a mother with an infant who'd had surgery on a cleft palate.''

"That was Adam's patient?''

"Yes.'' Kate recalled her surprise when she came into the room, seeing Adam cradling the baby in his arms. The picture had clung in her thoughts until the shooting. He'd looked so natural, so confident. She had wondered if he'd make a good father. The scene allowed her to witness Adam's tender side—one she'd never known.

"What next?''

"Señor Garcia. He had a knife wound from a street fight. He drank too much and used drugs. The day before he came to the clinic had been Venezuelan Independence Day so we'd already seen a lot of incidences from overindulgences that day and the day of the shooting.''

"Did you see Garcia leave the building?''

"I didn't notice.''

Sam scribbled her comment into a pad and spoke as if thinking aloud. "Far-fetched since Garcia probably isn't in Colorado Springs, but he might have connections.''

Kate couldn't imagine that.

"Same with the Clemente woman. Not likely but possible.''

"I don't think so,'' Kate said. "She was very religious. She just didn't seem the type.''

"Did she have a key to the dispensary?''

"She helped us stock medical supplies, but one of us usually opened the door and was there with her.''

Sam nodded. "Who speaks Spanish at the clinic?"

"We all do...a little. At least, enough to get by. When we had problems, we had Carmen help us out. If she wasn't there, Dr. Valenti spoke fluent Spanish. Usually we managed without help."

Sam bent his head over the notebook and recorded what she had said. "So give me the details again. You heard the shots."

Kate pushed her mind back again and brought out the details as she remembered them. Her pulse kicked up a notch as she recalled the blood and the fear that prickled her senses.

"Where were you at the time of the shooting?"

"In the reception area. I was in an office adjacent to the sign-in desk."

"That's located where?"

"Near the front door."

"Any other doors?" Sam asked, his pen posed over the notebook.

"The delivery door near the dispensary."

"So someone leaving would have passed you in the corridor or else exited through the dispensary door."

"Right. If they'd used the front door I would have passed one running out."

Sam made a note. "We'll assume they left the back way, then."

"I would think...and the body—the man Valenti shot—was in the back."

"Right. We received those reports from the Feds." He thought a moment, his eyes focused on the table-top. "Was the dispensary always well stocked?"

"Supplies came in regularly each month. We had

one delivery a month so near the end of that period we'd be running lower on meds.''

''They were delivered a certain week? Day?'' He tilted his head and waited.

''Usually the second Thursday of the month.'' She shrugged. ''I don't know why, but that's how it worked. That week, they were delivered on Tuesday—two days early. I'd finished stocking them that morning.'' She remembered the fiasco a few days earlier when she noticed the discrepancy in the inventory.

''So the new supplies arrived how many days before the break-in?''

Kate felt her eyebrows arch. ''That day. On Tuesday.''

''And if the drugs hadn't been delivered early that month, the looters would have found a short supply on Tuesday.''

''Right.''

He tapped the pen against his cheek. ''Interesting.''

''After we had the robbery attempt, I began to wonder if drugs had been taken before from the clinic.''

He straightened. ''What?''

Kate told him about the discrepancy she had found a few days before the burglary. At that time, she'd blamed herself for making an error, never thinking it could have been an earlier theft. ''We kept the medical supplies at the far end of the building, closer to the offices and near the delivery door. It was away from the examining rooms and nurses' desk. Unless we had a reason to be down there, it was usually a more deserted part of the clinic, especially on the late shifts when we had a smaller staff.''

Kate could see Sam's eyes snapping with possibilities. Before he could ask another question, the waitress arrived, and he slid the notebook into his pocket.

"I'll see how the pieces fit together, Kate. Thanks for going over this again. I know it's stressful to rehash it." His expression faded to a frown as he looked past her shoulder.

Kate glanced in that direction. To her pleasant surprise, she spotted Jessica Mathers. She eyed Sam again. His embittered look aroused her curiosity. "Do you know Jessica?"

He nodded, his gaze glued in her direction.

"I met her at the Galilee Women's Shelter." Kate looked back again, hoping to catch her eye. Jessica sat across from a well-dressed man. A wine bottle sat between them. She leaned toward him, her face animated and intense. The man's eyes didn't waver from hers. At the meeting, Jessica had mentioned she was a single mom. Could this older gentleman be the man in her life?

Sam's distraction bewildered Kate. "How do you know her?"

"She was involved in a car accident almost two years ago. I was the cop who answered the call. She was badly injured."

Kate reviewed the afternoon she'd met Jessica. "I didn't notice anything physically wrong with her when we met."

"I'm surprised. The accident was awful. She'd been injured. Her husband was killed, but her daughter didn't have a scratch. You never know."

Kate glanced at her again. "I had no idea."

"Apparently she hasn't changed since the night I

pulled her out of the wreckage. She still seems to be a party girl.''

Kate heard Sam's bitter tone and felt puzzled. ''What makes you call her a party girl?'' she asked.

''She's drinking. I would think with what happened to her she'd stay clear of alcohol.''

Kate didn't turn around again. She'd noticed a stemmed glass with something red. And the wine bottle. Could Sam be correct? He'd shocked her with his harsh comment. She focused on her burger and took a bite, but when she looked at Sam, he was still watching Jessica.

Chapter Thirteen

"How was your lunch with Sam?" Adam asked as Kate came through the door.

"Fine. He asked a million questions."

Kate beamed seeing Adam wide awake and sitting on the edge of his bed. Though his coloring had improved, an IV still dispensed medication. The bullet wounds followed by his infection, then the drug overdose had taken its toll, and Kate anguished, seeing him weak and vulnerable.

"What kind of questions?" Adam asked.

"Too many," she said, sitting beside him.

"I missed you."

She longed to be honest and tell him the same, but she couldn't. "You're feeling better."

"Yes...but I'd feel much better with you in my arms."

Before she could think, Adam drew her closer. His tender expression surprised Kate, and her heart thundered when she saw his lips part as he drew nearer.

She felt hers do the same, as if inviting him to kiss her. When his mouth touched hers, chills washed over her.

She knew he felt her shudder. He clasped her nearer while his own muted moan sang in her ears. Her eager lips moved on his, not wanting him to let go.

When he eased back, his gaze captured hers. "I feel much better now."

Kate was speechless at his unexpected behavior and her own. He'd held her hand, caressed her cheek and said things that confused her, but never had he kissed her.

Anxiety raced through her, and her protective wall rose. "I thought you wanted to hear about my lunch with Sam," she said.

His expression sparked with bewilderment. "Kate?"

She forced herself to look at him.

"Are you angry about the kiss?"

She couldn't lie, and honesty won out. "No...I loved it."

"Good," he said. "So did I."

"Do you want the answer to your question or not?" she asked. Her pulse raced, and she sounded breathless.

"I've forgotten it already." He gave her a teasing look, then nodded. "Yes. Tell me about your lunch with Sam."

She settled onto the chair for her own protection and detailed some of Sam's questions.

Adam's expression grew serious. "I've been think-ing about that day at the clinic. Today I recalled a weird disagreement I had with Dan Eckerd before I went in to see Señor Garcia. It came out of nowhere, and I had asked myself that day if we'd all been affected by a full moon."

"What happened between you and Dan Eckerd?" Kate asked, surprised to learn about this now.

Adam told her the story of Dr. Eckerd's reaction to the advice he'd given a patient. "It didn't make sense. I've never seen him fly off the deep end like that."

"I'm surprised, too, but we were all on edge that day. Maybe the Lord was warning us to beware?"

Adam slid his hand over hers and pressed it against his palm. "That day." He became silent a moment. "I keep getting visual flashes, but they leave too quickly. My hand on the dispensary door, two men, a face. It's frustrating. I think I'm about to remember and then it explodes and vanishes…like fireworks."

Her gaze drifted to his hand covering hers, but she managed to get her thoughts back on course. "Sam got me thinking, too. Something he asked me keeps niggling in my mind. Something that doesn't sit right, but I can't put my finger on it."

"Retrograde amnesia?"

She chuckled at his attempt to lighten the mood.

He raised her fingers to his mouth and kissed them.

Kate's pulse skittered at the pressure of his lips against her flesh. The sensation detoured their conversation and created new questions about their relationship. She felt uneasy with his attentiveness. It only spurred her longings, and what would happen when he was well and returned to the real world? Where would that leave Kate?

She withdrew her hand, then clutched both in her lap.

"You know, Kate," Adam said, "I've made a lot of mistakes in my life. I've paraded around like the prince of plastic surgeons, and I've come to realize it was my own fear of failure that made me that way."

"Fear of failure? You?" Kate felt a frown flash across her face. She couldn't imagine Adam afraid of failing.

"My dad had such expectations of us. You know how he is. He's a great father, but he demands excellence. I worked so hard to become a good surgeon, I forgot about being a person. I'd lost the skill somewhere along the way, so to cover my inadequacy, I became aloof. I pushed people away with my attitude rather than be rejected. But it didn't work. You didn't let it stop you from being a friend."

"Call me silly."

Instead of smiling, Adam frowned. "I'm being serious. Even though I goaded you, you gave me a look or comment and always bounced back. Your self-confidence was so much stronger than mine."

"Situations strengthen people. I had a difficult—" She stopped, realizing she'd nearly told him what she promised herself she would never reveal.

"You had a difficult…?"

Before Kate had to make up an answer, a noise sounded at the doorway and Dr. Emily Armstrong stepped into the room.

She smiled at Kate, then focused on Adam. "Hi, there. How are you feeling today?" She moved to his bedside. "I've heard about your problems."

"I suppose you could call them that."

"I'm so thankful that you're doing better, Adam. I wanted to see you earlier, but things keep getting in my way."

"No problem. I haven't been much of a host."

Emily sat on the empty chair and crossed her legs. "Kate told me about Doctors Without Borders. It sounds like a wonderful experience...except for your unfortunate ordeal. I'm thinking about it. One day, just maybe, I'll get the courage to be a little adventurous myself."

Kate listened while she spoke again of Peter and their problems. Kate wondered if Emily still loved her ex-husband. Could it be that God was still at work on their relationship?

"I need to stretch myself," Emily said. "I've avoided too many things in my life." She looked into the distance. "Do you think I'm too old to tackle something new?"

"You?" Adam grinned. "You'll never be too old."

"Thanks. I like to hear that." She rose. "I have to get back, but I wanted you to know I've been thinking of you." She patted his shoulder and headed for the doorway.

"Thanks," Adam said.

"Emily." Kate rose. "Could I walk with you for a minute?"

A puzzled look flashed across Emily's face, then vanished. "Sure."

Adam gave her a similar look.

Kate paused. "I'll be right back."

"Okay," he said, curiosity still etched on his face.

Kate followed Emily into the hallway. The need to

talk to someone had risen in her like a flame. She needed advice and someone who would listen.

"Problem?" Emily asked in the corridor.

"Not really...well, a little."

"What is it?" Emily asked.

Kate harnessed her internal turmoil and grasped her courage. She bit the inside of her lip, trying to drag the words to the surface. "It's Adam," she said finally.

Emily drew back, and her face paled. "You mean he's more ill than you've let on?"

"No. Not that. It's—"

"You can tell me, Kate. Has he done something wrong? I can't believe—"

"He's done nothing wrong. It's something right."

"I don't understand."

"Neither do I." Kate pulled the admission from her heart. "He's romantic. He held my hand, and he kissed me." She looked into Emily's eyes. "And I kissed him back."

Laughter burst from Emily's throat. "Oh, Kate, you had me so frightened, and you're telling me something wonderful."

"But it's not. I'm afraid. I know our relationship is only temporary. I've been by Adam's side through this whole ordeal. He thinks I saved his life, and he's grateful. Once he's healthy and—"

"Why are you afraid of love?" Emily took Kate's arm and led her to the window at the end of the hallway. "Love is a gift. It's nothing to fear."

"But we're from two different worlds." Kate unlocked her silence and poured out the story of her childhood. "It's not a pretty picture. How could I explain this to Adam?"

"Kate, love has nothing to do with that. It has to do with people who share a mission. You and Adam both want to help people in need. If you love to be with him and he makes your heart sing, that's all that matters. Don't worry about the past. It's the past, not the present."

"I wish you were right, Emily. I know Adam. I've seen his arrogance...."

Kate fell back against the wall for support. She had seen Adam's arrogance in the past but not recently. Adam had changed. The reality settled over Kate like gossamer. Soft and subtle, a gauzy truth that made reality seem unreal.

"Remember. Bad things can lead to good. You learned from your past. You worked hard. Adam sees who you are today. Remember, out of ashes, truth is born. Give Adam a chance."

Emily opened her arms, and Kate entered her embrace, longing to believe that Emily had spoken the truth.

Kate stood in the church parking lot and gazed up at the red roof and the tall square bell tower. She had passed Good Shepherd Christian Church many times but had never been inside. Today, she would be.

Perplexed about her life, Kate needed focus and comfort. She was falling in love with Adam, one of the most unwise decisions her heart had made. Wisdom assured her it was hopeless.

She'd tossed her rationalization from one side to the other, trying to explain what was happening be-

tween them. Adam had been wonderful to her since
their return...even romantic for a man confined to a
hospital, but his feelings couldn't be real. Adam came
from wealth and prestige. Kate came from poverty
and mediocrity. The two didn't mesh.

Kate ascended the steps into the massive church,
asking herself why she had come here rather than her
own congregation. Liza's invitation, perhaps. She'd
grown fond of Liza—a woman with a loving heart,
an open mind and a spirited soul. She was a giver,
and Kate admired her.

The summer heat cooled as Kate stepped into the
interior of the building. The organ's pipes resonating
into the entrance beckoned Kate to step into the sanc-
tuary. Ahead of her, a stained-glass window glowed
in the mid-July morning sun, the colors vibrant and
dramatic and amazingly similar to the stained-glass
window in the Vance Memorial chapel. She wondered
if the artist was the same.

She made her way halfway down the aisle and settled into a pew. Her gaze returned to the window
where Jesus, the Good Shepherd, stood holding a
lamb in his arm. He clasped a shepherd's staff in the
other hand, His face serene and loving. The picture
warmed her thoughts. Even when sinners strayed, Jesus sought the lost and brought them back to safety.
Kate needed to remember that.

Too often she struggled and drifted, loving the
Lord, but forgetting to praise or call on His name in
times of trouble. "The Lord is my shepherd. I shall
not want." The promise drifted through her mind like
a balm.

She drew her gaze from the window and scanned

the congregation, looking for the Montgomerys. The church offered two services, and she wondered if they attended the other. When she was about to give up her search, Kate spotted Frank Montgomery's impressive form and white hair on the left a few rows ahead of her. Liza sat at his side.

When the organ ceased, the pastor—Gabriel Dawson, the sign outside had said—stepped before the congregation, a good-looking African-American man with a strong build and a warm smile reflecting in his black eyes. "In the name of the Father, the Son and the Holy Spirit."

"Amen." The voices boomed and resonated from the spacious ceiling.

Kate bowed her head for the prayer, her own prayers rising for strength and acceptance of God's will. When the litany ended, Kate settled back for the scripture reading.

"The Bible reading for today comes from Romans eight." As he opened the large leather Bible, Pastor Dawson's rich voice filled the room. "Verses twenty-six and seven," he said. "'In the same way, the Spirit helps us in our weakness. We do not know what we ought to pray for, but the Spirit himself intercedes for us with groans that words cannot express. And he who searches our hearts knows the mind of the Spirit, because the Spirit intercedes for the saints in accordance with God's will. And we know that in all things God works for the good of those who love Him, who have been called according to His purpose.'"

The words washed over Kate like bathwater, warm, soothing, pure. "God works all things for the good of those who love Him." Where was her trust? Her faith? She had to let go and let the Lord's will be done in her life.

She thought back to when Adam was in the depth of pain, and she had been so filled with fear. She had not remembered that the Spirit felt her pain, groaned with her hurts and interceded on her behalf.

Kate captured the thought and held it against her chest, repeating the message. The Spirit felt *her* pain and *her* fears. God would be faithful to His promise to work good things in her life, so why did she continue to fear the past and worry about what people might think? God had been so faithful, so good, and Kate needed to cling to those words.

When the choir rose, Kate leaned back to enjoy the music, but before her back hit the pew, she jolted upright, seeing Sam Vance among them. He sat behind a keyboard, ready to play. Sam in a church choir. The image was ludicrous, but absurd or not, she watched him, lifting his voice in song to praise the Lord. The congregation swayed to the spirited rhythm, and Kate focused on the meaningful message as she listened to the song about God's goodness.

After the service ended, Kate held back to catch the Montgomerys. Liza spotted her as Frank headed off in another direction. The woman's eyes widened and her cheeks brightened with her greeting.

"Kate," she said. "Welcome. I'm so pleased to see you. What brings you to Good Shepherd?"

"Your invitation," Kate said, "and the need to spend some time with the Lord."

Liza opened her arms and gave her a hug. "You've been through so much," she said in Kate's ear.

Though surprised at her display of affection, Kate reveled in the warmth of her arms. "You, too."

"Are you in a rush?" Liza asked, loosening her grasp.

The question caught Kate off guard. "Not really. I have to work this evening. Did you need a lift?"

"Frank has a meeting, but I can wait. It should be short." She fiddled with her handbag a moment before continuing. "No. I wanted to talk with you for a moment."

Concern prickled up Kate's arms. "Talk? I have a few minutes." She pointed to the entry. "Here?"

"We could walk outdoors. It's a lovely day."

"That's fine," Kate said, following her lead to the exit.

"I told Frank I might be outside waiting. Let's find a bench."

As they stepped through the doorway, the sun's rays warmed the chill that Kate had felt earlier. She harnessed her concern, pushing God's words forward in her thoughts. "God works for the good of those who love him." Why was she so afraid? What could Liza ask that she couldn't handle?

Liza guided her into the church gardens. In the sunny spot, flowers blossomed in profusion, and along the walk aspen and mountain ash freckled the area with shade. Liza motioned to a bench while Kate followed her.

"It's lovely out here," Liza said.

Kate agreed, still wondering why Adam's mother had asked her to talk.

Liza set her handbag on the bench between them.

"Are you making any progress on those telephone calls for Jessica?" Liza asked.

"I have, and I'm doing well, if I do say so myself. I've added a few donations to the list…and a couple of requests to call back after they've had time to think about it."

"Good for you." Liza shifted her bag to the far side of the bench and closed the space between them. "I'm an older woman, Kate. Some of my senses have faded a little. I don't see as well as I used to, and my hearing isn't as sharp as it was, but I do see and hear things with my heart."

Kate held her breath. Should she admit she loved Adam? She was sure that's what Liza was about to ask. She almost grinned at the woman's persistence.

"When I asked you to help out at the shelter, I had no idea the project would touch you as personally as it's done."

Kate's breathing became laboured. "What do you mean?" she asked, knowing the answer.

"Some of your comments, the look on your face, let me know that the shelter has a deeper meaning to you than you want to let on. I'm sensing that something has caused you deep sorrow…and if you'd let me, I'd like to listen."

"But I don't—"

Liza shook her head. "Weeks ago you made reference to the Montgomerys' history and contribution. You said we live in two different worlds. I want to know about your world, Kate, because I think it's holding you back from wonderful things. Indulge an old woman, dear, please."

Kate repressed her panic. Her chest ached with the

desire to unlock her heart and release the details of her past that had rooted her in fear.

She studied Liza's gentle face. The tender look in her eyes ended Kate's lifelong struggle.

"It's so difficult to talk about." Her hands shook as she fiddled with her shoulder bag strap. "Times were so hard, and my mother did all she could to make a life for us…but life was against her."

Kate searched Liza's face and saw nothing but interest. "My father left my mother when I was very young. They were divorced, I suppose, and my mother raised me alone. She had many health problems, cancer at the root of most of them. I told you my mother died of cancer when I was eighteen."

"Yes, you did," Liza said, her gaze never wavering.

Kate couldn't maintain eye contact. The hurt was too deep and the shame was bottomless. "My mother's health kept her from holding a steady job, and we lived on welfare most of the time. We scrounged meals where we could, and we even stayed in homeless shelters more than once." She lifted her gaze to Liza's. "That's what you heard in my voice and saw in my eyes…experiences we've been discussing about the shelter that are too similar to the ones that I lived."

"But you shouldn't feel ashamed of that, Kate. Your mother did the best she could under the circumstances and that's all you could expect. She gave you a strong faith and a big heart. Sometimes the Lord allows us to suffer and cope with harrowing experiences to make us stronger people and to teach us humility and compassion. You have both of those, my dear.''

"I've never blamed my mother or the Lord. I realize it's part of life. We never know what we might be dealt. I survived. I struggled, but made my way through college. Yet somewhere inside me, I'm still the frightened child sleeping in a homeless shelter with an ailing mother. Self-esteem is based on worth, and I've always felt unworthy.''

"Kate, I see nothing but an intelligent, caring woman whose charm and beauty have captured my son's heart. He won't say it, but I see it in his eyes.''

Holding back tears, Kate closed her eyes, listening to Liza's hopeful words.

"Adam has always been my difficult son," Liza continued. "The one who I know so little about, but one I love with all my heart. It would bring me great joy to see you and Adam fall in love.''

"I've never told Adam a thing about me, Liza." Kate's words were a whisper. "He doesn't know about my life, living on handouts and in homeless shelters. I don't know that I can ever tell him.''

"I told you once before that rich or poor means nothing." She clutched her hand against her breast. "What counts is in here, Kate, and I believe that Adam has seen your heart. He admires you not only for your lovely appearance but for the deeper beauty inside.''

Liza lowered her hand and clasped Kate's. "I can promise you this. Your past will make no difference to my son. That's all I'm going to say.''

She drew Kate's hand to her chest. "We are equal in God's eyes, and what counts is right in here.''

The tears Kate had tried to harness flowed from her eyes and dripped from her chin. She'd longed for a mother for so long, and today she'd found one in Liza.

Chapter Fourteen

Monday morning, Kate sat in Adam's kitchen and sipped her coffee. So much had happened in the past two weeks. Events to fill a lifetime. And so much had happened between her and Adam. She feared thinking about it.

Her emotions swung from ecstasy to despair. She'd listened to Liza and wanted to believe her, but was it only a mother's wish and not reality? For now she clung to every minute with Adam, and if Liza was wrong, Kate would leave Vance Memorial. How could she spend days seeing Adam, remembering the emotion she'd felt in his arms, and have him walk past her as if she were a stranger?

And it could happen.

Kate jumped at the telephone's peal. Her heart pounded without reason as she reached to answer it. Hearing Adam's voice alarmed her.

"Anything wrong?" she asked.

"No, I want some real clothes. At least sweatpants."

"What's this all about?"

"I'm tired of this hospital getup. Can you bring my things with you today? I thought I had a shirt and pants here but they're missing."

"Your mom took the clothes home to wash them," Kate said, thinking back to Liza's display of motherly love.

"Then she must have my wallet and comb...the things from my pockets?"

Feeling calmer, Kate agreed. "I can pick them up for you if you want."

"Would you?"

Her body warmed hearing his requests, as if she were the special person in his life. Like a wife. She slammed the thought into her mental wastebasket. Cling to the moment, she reminded herself. "Sure. It's not a problem. I'll be there in an hour or so."

When Kate replaced the receiver, she leaned against the kitchen counter and pulled herself together. Her feelings for Adam had multiplied tenfold since the shooting. She'd grown protective and too involved. Too much for a friend. She was fooling no one about her feelings. She hadn't fooled Liza or Sam for that matter and...especially Adam, and he had just naturally joined in the amusement.

Time will tell. The words rang in her head like a death knell. Adam grew stronger every day. Soon he'd be out of the hospital. His life could move on to his country-club world and his better-than-thou attitude she'd seen so often.

And where would she be?

Forcing the concerns from her mind, Kate took her coffee mug into the bedroom. She dried her freshly washed hair, applied makeup, then dressed. Ready, she entered Adam's bedroom. Her breathing accelerated as she stood in the doorway, feeling like a voyeur. Though uncomfortable, she ambled to his closet and located a pair of sweats. A duffel bag sat on the floor, and she dropped them inside.

She looked in his dresser drawer and pulled out socks, but her hand trembled as she located his underwear in the drawer beneath. Too intimate. Too telling. Slimline boxers. Beige, pale blue or white. Like Adam, reserved and indifferent. Nothing too colorful or too exotic.

A robe hung on the closet hook, and she placed that in the bag with the other items. She zippered it closed, then headed downstairs to call the Montgomerys to tell them she'd be by for Adam's personal items.

The Monday late-morning traffic moved freely, and Kate arrived at the Montgomerys' home in good time. With each visit, the lovely home punctuated her awareness of different worlds and different lifestyles. Nothing could change that truth.

Before she reached the porch, Liza pulled open the door, her smile as warm as the morning air.

"Come in, dear." She stood back, motioning Kate to enter.

"I can't stay," Kate said, knowing Liza would try to feed her or invite her to visit for a while.

Liza ignored her statement and steered her into the breakfast nook. "I'm finishing brunch. Have some juice, at least." She poured a glass of orange juice before Kate could decline.

With little choice, Kate sank into the chair and accepted the beverage.

"Adam's doing so well," Liza said. "I'm hoping he'll be released soon."

The statement jolted Kate. She'd gotten so comfy at Adam's town house, she'd foregone looking for her own temporary housing. With Adam's release, she would need a place to live. "Yes, he does look well. He sounded like his old self this morning."

Liza smiled. "When he realized he was missing his wallet, I knew he's almost recovered."

Kate swallowed the last of the juice and slid back the chair to rise. Before she stood, Frank's voice bellowed from the living room.

Liza bolted upward and dashed to the doorway. "What is it, Frank?" She gave Kate a concerned look and headed down the hallway.

Kate followed, her own worry rising.

Adam's father sat in a recliner in front of the television. A newscaster's words were lost in Frank's tirade.

"Calm down," Liza said. "Tell us what's wrong."

Frank slapped his hand against the chair arm and hit the remote.

The silence rang in Kate's ears.

"Alistair Barclay has announced his candidacy for mayor in the next election."

Frank's face was bloodred, and Kate feared a stroke. She'd heard his irritation with Mr. Barclay in the past but knew little about the depth of the problem.

"He's a Brit. How can he run for mayor?" Frank said, his hands balled into fists. "The man is double-dealing. He's got something up his sleeve. Why mayor?" His eyes narrowed.

"I don't know, dear. I suppose he has issues," Liza said.

"I've got issues," Frank said, his voice blustering.

Kate held back her thoughts, wanting to tell him that Alistair Barclay was a nationalized citizen, but she felt out of place doing so.

"He's out to get me. That's it…but why?"

The front door opened on Frank's question, and Jake appeared at the living room archway. He looked at his father's face. "I just heard it on the car radio."

Frank's expression altered seeing his son, but he continued his comments about Barclay.

"He must be a citizen, Dad," Jake said.

Kate's head nodded before she could stop herself.

Jake noticed. "Is he, Kate?"

Kate wanted to kick herself for getting involved. "Colleen mentioned it the other day when she was telling Adam about her conversation with Sam. She said she recalled a feature story in the paper when he was naturalized." She swallowed, waiting for Frank's angry comments.

But Frank was silent.

"Guess the news left that out, Dad." Jake sat on a nearby chair and rested his elbows against his knees, his hands folded in front of him. "I don't think he'd win an election anyway."

"Why not?" Frank asked. "He seems to have a growing following. I hear he's donating money to every worthy cause in the city. You can't tell me those people won't support him."

"They might accept his money for the cause, but it doesn't mean they would vote for him as mayor. You've been a popular mayor, Dad. Good things have happened in Colorado Springs. Everyone knows that.''

"It's not the point, Jake."

A hush fell over them.

"What do you mean?" Jake asked.

"I'd decided not to run next term."

Liza let out a gasp. "Not run? But why?"

"I'm tired, Liza." His voice had softened and stress weighted his tone. "I've done what I can for the city. I'd like to see some new blood. New ideas."

"But what would you do, Dad?" Jake's back had stiffened like a flagpole.

"Something worthy. I was asked to run for president of the congregation at Good Shepherd…and I've thought about some charities I'd like to support."

Disappointment sounded in his voice, and Kate wondered if she should quietly leave the family discussion, but she felt trapped.

"You can't give up now," Jake said. "Who else could beat the guy but you?"

Frank shrugged. "Someone…I hope." He rubbed his face with the palms of his hands and stared into space. "This needs thought and prayers."

"You've got mine," Jake said.

Liza nodded, and Kate murmured her support.

Prayer. The good Lord must feel barraged by all His children's needs. Lately, Kate had sent up many for herself.

He stared out the window, his fingers twitching thinking of his newest plan. Montgomery was looking healthier and soon his memory could return and then…

He had to do something and fast. He couldn't use

the same technique he used last time. They were on to him now. If the sweet Nurse Darling hadn't rescued Montgomery, the torment would be over. The man would be dead, and he'd be free, but Montgomery lived and now he had to devise another method of removing the esteemed doctor from his life.

This time he'd thought it through more carefully. Why ask someone else to do the job when he could easily do it himself? One powerful injection of procainamide hydrochloride, and death would come immediately. Cardiac arrest, they would diagnose. Poor Montgomery had been under stress. His heart just wasn't strong enough to handle all the setbacks. Too bad the fine surgeon had to die.

He muffled his laughter. All he had to do was distract the officer outside Montgomery's door, and it would be over. One injection, and he'd be free.

And Montgomery would be dead.

Adam stood beside his bed and slipped one arm into the robe Kate had just brought from home. The sense of well-being engulfed him. Kate and his own clothing. It all felt so good. "Thanks for bringing my things, Kate." He tied the belt while one arm remained out of the sleeve. "I hope this IV comes out today. That will be a gift."

She stood at the foot of his bed, watching him, and his heart skipped seeing her sweet smile. "Dad said he'd come to see me today, so I'm sure I'll hear the Barclay story again." He could picture his father's frustration. Barclay had become a Montgomery enemy in the past couple years. "I'll have to remind Dad he's in a hospital so he'll keep the volume down."

"I think the neighbors heard him today even with the houses acres apart."

When she stepped nearer, Adam pointed to the privacy curtain. "Would you slide that closed for a minute?"

A scowl settled on her face. "Sure. Want me to leave?"

"Leave?"

"I thought you were going to put on your sweatpants or something."

"No."

A puzzled look replaced her scowl, and she turned and closed the curtain. Adam moved one step toward her but found himself restricted by his IV tubing. When she looked back, he beckoned to her. "Come here."

She tilted her head and stepped nearer.

He reached for her with his free arm and drew her closer. For the first time, he felt her body fully next to his. "We've never stood together like this."

Her eyes searched his. "No. You've been sick."

"But not anymore," he said.

Adam slid his arm around her back and pressed her to him. He could feel her chest moving against his, her breathing ragged, her breath whispering against his neck.

He tilted her chin upward, her mouth so close, and the fragrance of oranges and sweetness filled the air. He reveled in her smile, her well-shaped mouth and white even teeth that made his heart ache with longing. She gazed at him now, her rosy lips parted in question.

His longing grew, and he lowered his mouth to hers, drinking in the warmth. Standing beside her, he controlled his yearning to explore her soft form. He knew what God expected, but he'd waited so long to feel the sensations that moved through him. He'd waited forever to find someone like Kate.

Her body trembled beneath his grasp, and his own knees weakened until he eased back and caught his breath. "You're wonderful. I can't believe I let so much time pass before I realized how special you are."

"I'm not special. I'm very ordinary," she said, stepping away. "Don't make me something I'm not."

Her comment set him back, and he searched her face to understand. "If you'd look at yourself through my eyes, you'd know how really unique you are."

She touched his cheek, and for a moment, he feared she would cry. Tears pooled on her lashes, and the look depressed him. He drew her closer, wanting to wash away her fears and understand what made her so afraid.

"Anybody home?"

Adam pulled back as the curtain rustled open and Sam stepped through. "Sorry. Did I interrupt?"

His smug look made Adam smile. "Nothing that can't be repeated later."

Kate's cheeks glowed as she slipped her bag over her shoulder. "I need to get moving. I have to stuff envelopes at the women's shelter."

"Stuff envelopes?" Adam said.

"For the fund-raiser. Your mom will be there." She turned to Sam. "You didn't get roped into this thing, did you?"

Sam hesitated, a curious look on his face. "What thing?"

"The silent auction."

"Me? A silent auction?" He gave her an over-my-dead-body look. "You've got to be kidding. Auctions aren't my kind of thing."

"Just checking," she said, sending him an amused look. She turned to Adam. "See you later."

He captured her hand and kissed her fingers. "I won't be happy until you do."

Her surprised gaze shot from Adam to Sam and back before she slipped through the curtain and left.

"I've been trying to figure you two out." Sam hit the side of his head with his palm. "You are smitten," Sam said, sinking into the chair.

"I am." No argument. No denying it. "How's life?"

Sam shrugged. "Heavy-duty right now."

"This case?" Adam's pulse skipped at the look on Sam's face.

"Right. We're very concerned for your safety."

"Mine?" Sam's face didn't shift. No smile. Nothing but sheer concern. "You're not kidding."

"I'm not. It doesn't take a rocket scientist to figure out the overdose."

"What do you mean?"

Sam shrugged. "Don't worry about it."

"It was an error...wasn't it?"

Sam didn't respond.

"What do you think...?" Adam's stomach knotted. "You're sure this wasn't a medical error?"

"Sorry, friend. We're still keeping a guard outside your room, but one of these days you'll be released and we're going to have a difficult time keeping an eye on you...unless we put the pieces together before that. I've called my brother Travis, and we're going to meet. I think I need a private investigator's take on what I've found…just to be sure I haven't missed something."

"It's that bad?"

Sam gave him a single nod. "Tell me. Do you have any enemies here? Anyone you can think of?"

Adam shook his head. He wasn't everyone's best friend, but he'd never known any obvious animosity. Then Eckerd came to mind. "Just before the incident at the clinic I had a strange altercation with Dan Eckerd. He's a pediatrician. I've never seen him behave like that before." Though Adam told Sam about the incident, he was dead sure Eckerd wouldn't harm a fly…not even a jejen.

Sam pulled out his notebook and wrote down the name. "I'll see what I can find out about him. You never know."

When the curtain slid back, Adam's father strode into the room. He looked tired and stressed. Sam rose and offered him the chair, but he declined and sat on the edge of Adam's bed.

"Bad day, Dad?"

Sam settled back in his chair.

Frank nodded, and as Adam suspected, he retold the story Adam had already heard from Kate.

"I didn't know you'd decided not to run for mayor," Adam said, surprised to hear that. Kate hadn't mentioned it. "I don't think it's a good idea. You're a great mayor."

"You sound like Jake." He gave Adam's arm a pat. "That's where my thoughts were, but I may have to reconsider. I'll see how things go."

He looked toward Sam. "How are you these days?"

Sam shrugged. "Sounds like you have your hands full enough for both of us."

Adam appreciated Sam not going into his suspicions with his father. No sense in making him worry, too.

"I learned something about Barclay a couple days ago," Sam said. "He's connected somehow with a construction company called El Rey. Travis ran across that piece of information. That's the group that's been putting up his hotels."

"El Rey," Frank said, surprise showing on his face. "I thought it was Elroy. No wonder I'd never heard of the company...and you mean to tell me Barclay has his fingers in that pie, too?"

"Seems so."

Adam watched the two men pause in silence, their brows furrowed. "What's that mean?"

"Doesn't make sense," Frank said.

Sam shrugged. "I just thought you'd like to know."

Frank gave him a wide-eyed look while Adam still felt in the dark.

"Why take bids if you own the company and know you'll give the bid to yourself?" Frank muttered.

The question traveled through Adam's mind. He was sure Sam knew more than he was saying. "Maybe he doesn't own the company. He could be on the board of directors or it could be owned by a conglomerate."

Frank shook his head. "Nothing makes sense to me."

Adam eyed Sam, who stayed noncommittal. "I'm guessing Barclay didn't want anyone to connect him to El Rey…so he put the jobs up for bid. That's the only thing that made sense to me."

His father only wagged his head and looked disheartened.

Adam's mind kicked out a thought. "Do you know what El Rey means?"

The two men shook their heads.

"The King," Adam said, using a little of the Spanish he knew. "Maybe Barclay thinks he's the king of construction."

Frank uncoiled his arms and rose. "I'm too frustrated to laugh." He stepped toward the doorway. "I have a meeting this afternoon so I need to get going. Good to see you looking so well, son." He shook Adam's hand, then Sam's.

"Thanks, Dad," Adam said, rising as his father stepped toward the curtain.

Sam rose, too, and moved toward the doorway. "I have work to do, too. I might as well walk out with your dad."

"Sure," Adam said, surprised at his quick departure.

"I'm praying we get something solid soon," Sam said, vanishing through the doorway.

In the empty room, Adam felt more alone than he'd ever felt in his life. Did he have any enemies? He'd never really thought about it until now.

Chapter Fifteen

"You're looking good, Adam," Gordon Reese said. "Your incision is nearly healed, and I see you're off the IV."

"Finally," Adam said.

"Fletcher says your getting stronger," Reese continued. "As far as I'm concerned, you can be released whenever he thinks you're ready."

"Released." Adam put his hands behind his head and stretched his neck forward. "That sounds good, Doc. I'm ready."

"Don't jump the gun. Fletcher's the last one you have to convince you're ready to head home."

Adam lowered his hands and rolled over on his side. "I appreciate all you've done, Gordon. You've been with me through this whole thing."

The surgeon grinned. "I sure have. How's the memory? Any flashes of remembrance?"

An eternal question. It grated on Adam's nerves. "None yet. But I'm hopeful."

"Sometimes it takes months. I'm confident it'll all come back."

"Glad you are." A movement caught his eye, and Kate came through the doorway.

"Gordon," she said, stepping beside him. "Isn't it late for you to be here?"

"Emergency surgery. I tried to find a minute earlier, but there's been too much excitement coming back here and then slipping right back into work without a break. I finally grabbed a moment and snuck up to see Adam." He patted Kate's shoulder. "He's looking good and should be out of here soon."

Kate's smile brightened Adam's mood. She'd acted so natural the past few days, and it had increased his hopes for a relationship once he was released.

Reese stepped toward the door. "I'll let you rest. Glad you're doing so well. You've been through so much." He shifted his gaze. "See you, Kate."

She waved, and Adam watched him move into the hall while his thoughts lingered on his release and on Kate.

"I came in to turn off your light. Now that I'm back at work, I can order you around. Time for patients to sleep," Kate said, reaching over him to push the button. He grasped her hand, and in the dark, she leaned down and brushed a kiss on his lips.

She startled herself. She'd kissed Adam Montgomery. Her pulse galloped at the realization, and she moved to step away, but Adam captured her hand again and drew her closer.

"Was I dreaming or did Nurse Darling kiss me?"

"You were dreaming," she said, hearing her voice breathless in the hush of the room.

He chuckled and clasped her shoulder, urging her toward his mouth. His lips parted, and the second kiss was powerful, leaving her gasping.

She eased back. "There's a police officer outside. I may have to call for help."

"Me, too," he said, letting her hand go. "You can't escape me, Kate. I'll send the posse after you…or Brendan. I think he's on duty tonight."

She agreed. It was Brendan. "You need your rest. Go to sleep."

"How can I sleep after that?" he asked, rolling over on his side and happy for the first time since he'd been in the hospital, relieved that his IV had been removed. He tucked the now-untethered arm under his cheek and rejoiced with his new freedom.

He stood inside the janitor's closet and peeked through a chink in the doorway. He'd had to wait for the quiet. Patients' lights had ceased their flashing in the hallways, nurses' shoes padded along the tile floor and the incessant intercom had quieted for the night.

Most patients were asleep by now. Laughter came from the nurses' station as they eased back, letting the night settle in. He could hear their voices like a hum in the hallway. Most didn't stir unless a patient rang the call button, but he was prepared for that.

He had the diversion ready, the syringe in his pocket. Enough cc's to do the job. He'd thought long and hard how to distract the officer outside Montgomery's door, and he had the perfect plan.

His pulse raced, and his heart kicked in his chest as he pulled out the lighter. One flick and the innocent fire burning in a janitor's bucket would cause a little stir. He could slip past without notice.

He steadied himself, willing his mind and body to work as one. He could handle danger, but he needed anonymity. He chuckled to himself. Anonymity. The reason for his brilliant scheme.

One more look. The hall was quiet. He leaned down, flicked the lighter and ignited the saturated rags. The flame licked upward.

When he slipped into the corridor and closed the door, he managed to move with a steady gate toward the officer. His fingers trembled in his pocket gripping the syringe.

The officer gave him a nod.

He smiled, then paused, turned back and sniffed the air. "I think I smell something burning." He tilted his head down the hallway where he could detect a curl of smoke easing from under the door.

"I'm in a hurry," he said. "Would you mind checking?"

The officer looked concerned and headed down the hallway, his head lowered and his gaze obviously intent on the smoke seeping from below the doorway.

With the officer busy, he quickly doubled back and slipped into Adam's darkened room. His pulse thundered in his head, and his chest tightened with each breath. A few seconds and he'd slip out again, undetected.

Guardedly, he inched across the room, pausing long enough to hear Adam's steady breathing. Excitement rippled through his limbs. Once he'd given Adam the injection, he could have his own. His own euphoria. The loving barbiturates that offered him a taste of ecstasy.

He dug into his lab coat pocket and pulled out the syringe. His salvation was here in the liquid. He moved closer to the bedside, removed the needle's cap, placed his finger on the plunger and leaned forward.

"Oh! You scared me."

He jerked back and dropped the syringe into his pocket. "Just checking on the patient," he muttered, seething at the interruption. "I see he's sleeping."

The nurse who'd entered the room sometime after him backed away. "Yes. It's late," she whispered. "I didn't know anyone was in here. We had a small fire in the janitor's closet, and we're checking rooms for smoke."

Adam mumbled, then turned and lifted his head, his gaze directed at the nurse. "What's the problem?"

"Nothing. I didn't mean to wake you."

Adam shifted again, and his eyes widened. "What are you doing here?"

"I just stopped in to see how you're doing."

"Don't you think it's a little late?"

"I finally had a minute." His hands trembled as he headed toward the doorway.

Anger rolled through him. The stupid nurse. If she hadn't come in, it would have been Goodbye Montgomery.

"I'll see you tomorrow, Adam."

He hurried down the corridor, his mind jumbled with his thwarted plan.

"Good job, Doc," the officer said, standing outside the scorched closet door. The smoldering bucket had

been removed and only soot and ash remained. "If
you hadn't noticed the smell, the fire might have done
more damage. It could have been serious."

Holding in his frustration, he nodded to the man
and sped away, wanting distance between him and
the situation.

What would he do now? He needed Montgomery
dead.

And he would be.

Soon.

The next morning, Kate stood at Adam's hospital
room doorway and admired him sitting in the chair
near the window. Sunlight streamed through the glass
and bathed his pale skin with a warm glow. Though
he'd lost weight, he looked stronger.

Although stress continued to etch his handsome
face, he would soon be back to normal. Once released, he'd return to his life...and Kate to hers. Each
time the reality came, it filled her with a deep aching
loneliness.

"Hi," he said, looking away from the window.
"You look gorgeous today."

She glanced at her beige pants and rust-colored top
and would have chuckled had her earlier emotion
eased. She crossed the threshold. "I hope you slept
after that crazy fire scare. Weird, wasn't it?"

"Chemicals do odd things. Probably a floor cleaner
made friends with a disinfectant. You just never
know."

"But the fire—you can't tell me it's spontaneous
combustion."

"Why not? Stranger things have happened." He

twisted his head, and his gaze captured hers. "You don't think that—"

"No. I'm just nervous. Too much has happened lately."

A rap sounded on the door, and Kate turned her head. Dan Eckerd stood inside the doorway.

"I'm not interrupting anything, am I?" He gave them a curious look.

"No. Come in, Dan. How are you?" Kate asked.

"Great." He turned to Adam. "And you're looking better, more awake than the last time I saw you."

"I'm getting there. Thanks. Still weak, but it's to be expected."

The pediatrician rocked back on his heels. "I noticed you had a little excitement up here last night."

"You mean the fire?" Adam asked.

"Lucky no one was hurt," Dan said, crossing his arms over his chest. He gave Kate a quick look as if he were uncomfortable. "Listen, Adam, I want to apologize for my behavior back in Venezuela. I can't get it out of my head how badly I treated you. It was foolish."

"No need," Adam said. "We all make mistakes. I've made my share." He sent Kate a private look. "If I could take back the way I've behaved too many times, I'd do it in a minute."

Dan lowered his arms. "I appreciate your attitude. I've been wanting to let you know how sorry I am. I felt like a heel. Right after that happened you were shot and I know you've been through so much. Gossip spreads."

"I'm sure I've had my day on the hospital grapevine."

Dan shot a telling look toward Kate. "Yes, I suppose you have." He stepped forward and extended his hand. "I just wanted to let you know that I'm truly sorry."

Adam grasped his palm. "No grudges here, Dan. I'm too grateful to be alive."

"I bet. See you both later." He gave them a nod and headed through the door.

"That was a long time coming," Kate said.

"Yes, but like I told him, I'm not going to dwell on it." He wiggled his eyebrows. "I have other things on my mind."

"Like what?" Kate asked.

He didn't answer, but only grinned.

"Why the big smile?"

"Hmm? No IV," he said, stretching his arm out and swaying it in front of her.

"You had that out before today." She stayed across the room and sank on the edge of his bed.

He gave her a toying look and beckoned to her. "Maybe I'm happy because the doctor said I should be out of here in a day or two. I'm ready to leap from this building in a single bound." He chuckled at his superhero joke.

"You won't be doing much leaping for a while," Kate said. "But I'm glad for you. I know you're anxious to be home." Mixed emotions skittered through her. The time she'd been afraid to face had finally arrived. Adam's freedom.

"At least I'll be home." His expression let her know he understood his limits. "They tell me I'm not allowed to work for a while. Fletcher and Reese both want to make sure I have no lasting memory problems. I suppose they're hoping I'll remember what happened and ease their minds.''

"It'll ease yours, too," she said.

"It will." He motioned to her again. "What's on your mind? I see that look on your face."

"*That* look?" She covered her face, then pulled her hand away trying to be lighthearted, which was far from what she felt. "I'm facing my own reality. You'll be released soon, which means I need to find a place to stay. I'm in your town house, remember?"

"I remember. Sounds good to me." He grinned while his hand erased the air as if wiping away his comment. "Just teasing, Kate. That's not the kind of people we are."

His comment rattled through Kate's mind. What kind of people were they? Different. Opposite. Nothing in common.

"I have an easy solution," Adam said. "The doctors don't want me to be alone for a while until I'm stronger. I'll stay with my folks, and you can use the town house until you've found something else. How's that?"

"I can't do that. It's your home. I'll get a motel until I find an apartment…or maybe I can bunk with Emily."

Adam rose. "I won't hear of it. I'm not going back there until I'm stronger so you might as well stay at the town house." He moved to the bed and sat beside her.

Unable to handle the closeness, she shifted away.

"Why are you so standoffish?"

"I'm not standoffish," she said.

"You just moved away from me."

"I was making more room, that's all."

He slid his arm around her and drew her closer. "I don't want more room, Kate. I want to be with you." He leaned over to look into her face. "Do you understand what I'm saying?"

Kate couldn't respond without crying. She swallowed her tears while her heart tumbled through her chest.

"Please tell me what's wrong." He grasped her shoulders and turned her to face him. "I want to make something of our relationship. I've never been romantic, Kate, but I can try. I told you a few days ago that I was blind all these years. I never knew how special you are."

"Your eyes were wide open, Adam. You saw everything right. I'm not the woman for you."

He flinched with her words, but her comment didn't stop him. "Listen to me. I'd never seen what a beautiful person you are. I respected your work, but I missed the obvious."

He closed his eyes and shook his head. "Let me be honest. I *avoided* the obvious. When I was drawn to you, I did everything in my power to keep myself at a distance. Do you remember how I insisted on calling you Katherine? I did that for me, Kate."

She felt a tremor ripple through his body. The muscles in his arms twitched. "Your name was too sweet for me. Too intimate for the emotions I was feeling. I had my image—my protection—that aloof, arrogant side that covered my inability to show my feelings." He shook his head. "Don't ask me why. I couldn't tell you in a million years."

His plea rent her soul. Adam was all the man she'd

ever wanted, and he was offering her the fantasy she could only dare to dream. He'd said he wasn't romantic. Her mind soared to the wonderful ways he'd made her feel like a special woman—the caresses, the kisses, the sighs.

But it could never be. If she told him the truth, if he learned about her lowly beginnings, he would run as fast as his weakened legs could carry him to one of the rich society women who fit his lifestyle.

He said he admired her. Where would his admiration be if he knew she'd come from homeless shelters and wore hand-me-downs from strangers? She had to say goodbye. She opened her mouth, but she couldn't say the words.

"Is it me, Kate? Can't you forgive me for my egotism? I can only promise you that I've changed. For the first time in my life, I realize that God is the only power in my life. He's my only hope and strength in this world. No one can do it all alone, and no one can take credit for success because the Lord gave us the abilities, the gifts. It's as simple as that…and somehow I missed learning that in my spiritual journey."

His eyes pleaded, and his face revealed his hurt, but Kate could not find the courage to tell him the truth.

Lord, give me strength, she thought. *Help me to do Your will.* She listened for God's voice, but the clanging in her head wouldn't allow her to hear any sound but her own shame and panic.

"Thank you for the compliments, Adam. You're doing so well, and you'll soon be back working and enjoying yourself just as before." She felt his hands go limp and drop from where they'd gripped her shoulders.

His mouth opened to speak, but she cut him off.

"I'll take your offer to use the town house until I can find something. I hope it won't be more than a few days." She slid from the bed and out of his grasp. "I admire you so much, and I know your life will return to all that it's meant to be. So will mine. I'm thinking about leaving Vance Memorial. I heard some of the other hospitals have better benefits."

His mouth gaped, and his eyes sparked with disbelief. "You're changing jobs. You're thanking me for the use of my town house. You're ignoring my feelings for you. I thought you felt the same, Kate. I truly believed you cared as much about me as I do you."

"Wasn't it a game? Wasn't it something to fill your time until you were well? That's all I thought it was. I was going along with the gag." She slipped her bag over her shoulder. "I have to run."

"Kate, please…"

She was gone.

Adam stared at the empty doorway, his mind whirling with the past few minutes.

What had happened?

Game? He didn't know what she was talking about. He'd never been a game player. He hated games. He'd opened his heart and thought she felt the same. He'd seen her reticence at times. He'd sensed she was holding back. He'd wondered why, but…

Pain rushed through him worse than the wounds

he'd suffered earlier. She'd turned him down. He lay back on the bed as the ache coursed through him.

Ignored.

Rejected.

Chapter Sixteen

He covered his smile as he walked away from Montgomery's doorway. Great timing. He'd moved away before Kate exited, but he'd heard their plaintive love story. The argument. The goodbye. Montgomery had been rejected. He'd enjoyed nothing better in years.

With Montgomery healing and soon leaving the hospital, he needed to act. No more ineffective plans with injections. He needed something more powerful. He needed to get Montgomery out in the open, away from the hospital…and now he knew what the man would fight for. His smile broke free, and he let loose a laugh.

A passerby gave him a peculiar stare, and he only grinned back.

He only needed to give it a day's thought. He'd kept notes. He'd been watching and listening.

Yes. Now he knew what Montgomery would fight for—what he would give his life for.

And he would.

* * *

Adam had not slept. During the night, he paced his room, his mind whirring with tangled emotions. Anger, frustration, disappointment, love and fear boiled together, leaving him drained and bewildered. He sat on the corner of the bed, his head bowed, asking the Lord to soften Kate's heart and to let her know the truth. He loved her. He loved her more than life itself.

He watched the sunrise, then dialed his town house telephone number, praying for Kate to answer. He needed to explain the depth of his feelings. His answering machine picked up, and he spoke his message into the silence until it cut off.

Adam tried again and again all morning until he wanted to scream at God and ask Him what he should do. Why didn't the Lord intervene? He sank into the chair and gazed out the window, the bright sun smarting his grainy eyes. *Why, Lord?* He asked over and over.

How can I prove my love? How? What can I do to let her know I'm not a rich Romeo who'd been playing games with her? I'm so far from it.

He dropped his head into his hands, tears forming on his sleepless eyes.

"Adam?"

He lifted his head and saw Sam standing in the doorway, his face grim. "Something wrong?"

"I was going to ask you the same question."

Adam looked away, then had a change of heart. Why avoid the truth at this point? Sam knew already. "Yesterday I told Kate how I felt about her. I let her know I'd like to pursue a relationship with her. She walked out on me."

Sam's head flew back as if Adam had punched him. "She what? If I've ever seen a woman in love, it's Kate."

"That's what I thought. Something's not right."

Sam strode into the room and leaned his shoulder against the wall. "I'm sorry, Adam, and I'm afraid something else isn't right, either."

Sam's tone jarred him. "What do you mean?"

"Things are falling together, and they don't look good. We need to keep a close eye on you."

"On me? Why now?"

"You know something, Adam."

Adam looked at him in disbelief. "I do? And what is it?"

"That's what we need to find out. You must have recognized someone, or you've seen something you shouldn't during the robbery attempt. Someone is afraid you'll remember. You were shot there. Given a narcotic overdose here. Who knows how long before another attempt is made?"

Adam's frustration mounted. "So what can I do?" He slammed his fist against the mattress. "I don't remember a thing. I told you that."

Sam lifted his hand. "You can't do anything except be careful. We've beefed up security. I just sent people over to keep an eye on the town house."

He hesitated so long it caught Adam's attention.

"And I'm worried about Kate, too," Sam said finally.

"Kate?" Adam's heart squeezed in a vise. "Why would you say that?"

"I've been calling her all day," Sam said.

"So have I," Adam admitted. "She should be here

any time." He glanced at his watch. "In fact, she's—"

"Late. I just asked at the desk. She didn't show up today."

"I know it's—"

A buzz sounded, and Sam held up his hand to stop his sentence. Sam grabbed his pager and eyed the readout. "This might be important." He pulled a cell phone from his pocket and then dropped it back in. "Can't use the cell here. I'll catch a pay phone."

Adam watched Sam hurry through the door while unexpected terror slithered through his limbs like tentacles.

In moments, Sam returned and crossed to Adam's side. "Kate's been driving your car, right?"

Adam's mind twisted and knotted. "Yes. I told her to use my slot at the hospital."

"The car's here, but she's not, Adam."

"Kate. No." Panic turned to terror. Reasonable possibilities tore through his mind. She'd gone out with one of the nurses after work last night and left the vehicle behind. She was so angry she didn't use his car. "Maybe there's an explanation. Maybe she—"

"We'll do everything we can." He gripped Adam's shoulder. "I have to go, Adam, but before I leave, I have one more question."

One more question? What about Kate? Adam felt brain dead. Tears knotted in his throat and pushed behind his eyes. "What is it, Sam?"

The telephone's ring caused them both to jump. Adam stared at his phone, praying it was Kate. He reached across the space, his fingers trembling, and grasped the receiver. "Hello." His voice sounded hollow.

He strained to listen to the muffled sound. "I can't hear you." He pushed the receiver to his ear. Horror filled him, but he hid it from Sam. "Yes. I understand." The distorted voice gave him instructions. His mind froze. He couldn't think. Nothing made sense. "Yes. All right." Someone had kidnapped Kate. Adam clung to the phone, trying to calm himself before hanging up. He had to face Sam…and Sam couldn't learn the truth. He swallowed, then placed the telephone on the cradle.

"What's your question?" he asked, not making reference to the call.

Sam gave him a puzzled look. His eyes shifted from the telephone to Adam's face.

Adam needed time to think. He needed a plan. "The question, Sam." He rose and waited.

Sam's eyes shifted from the telephone. "In Venezuela, when you left the compound and came to the clinic, which door did you enter?"

Adam gazed at him dumbfounded. What did that have to do with anything? He searched Sam's serious face. "The front door."

"Why?" Sam asked.

"It was the closest."

"So if you were in a hurry, you'd come through the front door."

"I just told you that."

Sam nodded. "Thank you." He backed toward the door. "We'll find Kate. God willing, we'll locate her." He vanished into the corridor.

There was the crux. Was God willing?

Adam had no intention of leaving the job to Sam or the police department. A madman had Kate, and he'd been ordered not to tell anyone. He had no time to lose. Adam needed a plan...some way to get out of the room without alerting the officer outside his door.

He crumpled onto the edge of the bed, his prayer rising to heaven. *I can't do this alone, Lord. Help me find a way. I can't do it alone.*

He'd waited for the tourists to leave the area and for the coming darkness before he forced Kate up the white rock toward the cave entrance. The barrier stopped him from going inside, but boulders along the outcropping made good cover, and the dark night would help to hide them.

Kate had struggled when he surprised her in the hospital garage. No one had noticed him waiting, and when Kate realized he hadn't just stopped to chat, a few drops of chloroform on a handkerchief held to her nose did the trick. He put her in his car, and when he'd found a lonely road, he'd tied her arms and legs, then put a gag in her mouth before locking her in his trunk.

Now in the dusky light, he waited for Montgomery. He was sure he would come to save the sweet nurse. He chortled aloud at his cunning plan. Once he had become certain that Montgomery had fallen for Kate, it was all he'd needed.

He'd never really liked the doctor. His self-importance grated on everyone's nerves at times, but Montgomery's real downfall was that he'd been at the wrong place at the wrong time. If his memory fully returned, then he'd know too much.

Kate squirmed and grumbled beneath the tight gag, but he ignored her. The cloth kept the sounds quiet, and he rather enjoyed hearing her struggle. He'd watched how protective she'd become with Montgomery—hovering over him like a mother hen. She deserved to die, too, and she would, but only after she watched the proud doctor meet his death.

Adam slid on his shoes, then hiked up his too-large pants, amazed at the weight he'd lost. He prayed the Lord would be with him now as he made his move. But first, he had to get Brendan away from his room.

Ready, he tiptoed to the doorway and opened it an inch. "Brendan."

His cousin looked at him with surprise and rose from the chair beside the door. "Something wrong, Adam?"

"Yes and no. I'm okay, but my mouth is dry and I need some ice water. I've been buzzing the nurses for a half hour and no one's answered. Could you run down to the desk and tell them I need ice water?"

Brendan looked toward the nurses' desk, then back to Adam. "But I'm not supposed to leave my station. You know that."

"Come on. It's only fifty feet down the hall. I'd go, but I'm feeling weak. I'll be fine for one minute."

Brendan hesitated until he finally shrugged. "I suppose it'll be all right." He headed left toward the desk, and Adam waited a moment until he'd passed three doorways before he made his move.

With the corridor clear except for Brendan, he

slipped into the hallway and headed in the opposite direction. The emergency stairs were only a short distance away. He opened the door, hurried inside and took the stairs two at a time, glancing over his shoulder until he felt safe. When he reached the parking garage, as Sam had said, his car was still parked there.

He felt beneath the front panel until he located the small metallic box that hid his emergency key. He'd misplaced his remote, and the stored key had served as a lifesaver more than once. He slipped into the car seat, rotated the key and heard the engine turn over.

Without a moment's loss, he backed out of the slot and headed toward the exit. He slid his card into the meter slot and watched the arm raise. His heart thundered beneath his sweatshirt, and his damp palms gripped the steering wheel as he squealed out of the parking structure. Nothing could stop him. He needed to do this alone…just as the voice instructed him. Kate's life was at stake, and that was all he could worry about now.

Sam gaped at the receiver, not believing what he'd just heard. "What do you mean Adam left the hospital? How in the world did he manage that?"

Brendan hemmed and hawed until he admitted he'd left the door to ask the nurse for ice water.

"Ice water. I can't believe you fell for that, Brendan. Okay. Do this for me. Get down to the parking garage and see if Adam's car is there. His slot is marked, then let me know right away."

His mind raced as he hung up the phone. His thoughts flew back to his earlier visit to Adam's room and the telephone call. When Adam hung up he'd looked distracted. Sam had wondered at the time. Who had called Adam?

He pulled the case notes from his pocket and flipped through the information. He had proof that drugs had been stolen from Vance Memorial and from the clinic in Venezuela. His brother, Travis, was checking out hospitals where some Vance Memorial doctors had previously worked before going to Doctors Without Borders. If he learned drugs were missing from any of those hospitals, it could help point to someone here who was apparently involved.

He also suspected a connection between the Diablo Syndicate and the Venezuelan drug cartel, La Mano Oscura—the Dark Hand. He had nothing solid, but Sam sensed they were heading in the right direction. One day they would know for sure.

He'd mentally shifted the puzzle pieces together in every direction. Some pieces didn't make sense, but one did. The discrepancy had jumped out at him like a neon sign. Could he be right?

His phone rang, and Sam answered. Brendan's voice shot over the wire: Adam's car was gone. Sam jumped from the chair and slammed the phone onto the cradle. Now he had to find Adam.

Sam dashed to the dispatcher's desk and yelled for her to send out an APB to look for Adam's car. Where would he go? For Kate. Whoever called had lured Adam to his death by using Kate.

Adam evaded the stoplights and made a right turn onto Cimarron. Leaving the downtown area, the route became Highway 24. His destination: Garden of the Gods.

He hadn't been there in years, but he could never forget the towering red sandstone formations and their changing colors in the evening light. Ahead, between the trees, mountains rose in the distance, only a silhouette against the dusky light.

Adam turned off the highway and raced along Gardner Road into the park a few minutes before closing. Tension gripped his back as he drove the longer route so he could come in from behind the North and South Gateway rocks. His plan: creep up on the kidnapper without his knowing.

The sun had set by the time Adam came to a stop beside the huge red rocks. He had turned off his headlights before reaching his destination and now stared into the night. A crescent moon spread light over the formations, and as his eyes adjusted, he could see the white rock like a pale ghost rising ahead of him.

He needed to plan his moves. He had no weapon. Someone had shot him once. Why not again? Adam pressed his palms over his eyes and thought. Since he'd talked with Sam he'd been dazed by the telephone call. Adam hadn't taken time to think back to Sam's question. Now, it settled over him.

The quickest way into the clinic in Venezuela was the front door. It was the logical way for staff to enter from the living quarters. The body had been found at the back of the clinic. That's what he'd learned from Kate. Why had it taken him so long to realize the truth?

Pieces fell into place. If the logical way to enter the clinic was through the front, why had Valenti confronted the suspects at the delivery door?

Valenti. Bile rose to his throat. His colleague. An

internist who knew medication…who knew how to give orders over the telephone. Using another doctor's name was easy when talking to a new nurse. The truth rocked him.

Valenti looked ill and had gotten worse since Adam had known him. His face sagged, bags had formed beneath his eyes, which looked glazed as if he were…on drugs.

Drugs. The motivation. The goal. The evil that had taken a good doctor and destroyed him.

The night of the closet fire Valenti had appeared in his room. Adam's panic rose. Valenti had tried to kill him twice…maybe three times. He wouldn't hesitate again.

His hands trembled as he reached for the door handle. He could wait no longer or the man would become agitated and harm Kate before Adam had a chance to get to her. But what could he do?

The truth struck him. With no weapon and no vantage point, he could do nothing. He bowed his head, his eyes moist with tears. *Lord God, forgive my foolishness. I can't do this without You. You've promised to be faithful. You've promised strength and protection from evil. Father, I need Your help. I beg You in the name of Your most precious Son, Jesus.* ''Amen'' whispered in his mind and soothed his heart.

Blurred by tears, his eyes sought the shrouded white rock.

God was his strength.

Chapter Seventeen

Kate lay behind a boulder on the stony outcropping. Her face stung from the tape pulled tight across her mouth. The adhesive pulled and burned against her skin, and in fear, she struggled for breath.

Earlier, she'd awakened dazed and had struggled to open her eyes. When she'd gained consciousness, her mind spun with the details of what had happened.

Lionel Valenti had caught her in the hospital parking lot. He'd asked to speak to her and said he wanted to show her something. When she'd reached his car, he'd covered her nose and mouth with a cloth. The odor had sickened her. Chloroform, she'd guessed. That's all she remembered.

She'd awakened in his trunk, bound and gagged. The road bounced beneath her, the foul scent of exhaust fumes curled around her and nausea curdled in her throat. She'd lain there forever, it seemed. She'd known dusk was coming. Gray light had filled the cracks in the trunk lid. Her body had quaked with fear, as much for Adam as for herself.

Her mind had raged with anger at her stupidity. Why hadn't she realized who had done the horrible deed in Venezuela? Now images fell into place. She thought of the Bible verse that reminds Christians, now we see through a glass darkly until we meet face-to-face. The Bible promised God's face...not Lionel Valenti's, but the verse gave her hope. *God works for the good of those who love him.*

Finally the trunk lid opened and the unpredictable doctor had dragged her out, unbound her feet and forced her up the rock formation. At the top, he'd bound her again, his voice breaking into wild laughter. The glazed look in his eyes confirmed her suspicion of drug use. Now, she understood the dispensary theft. Lionel Valenti had stolen drugs before— from Vance Memorial and others, he'd told her, hissing the story into her face.

As the last color faded from the sky, she'd listened to his crazed telephone call to Adam, muffled by a cloth stretched over his cell phone. Lionel Valenti carried a gun and from this vantage point, he had a direct shot. Shock and disbelief tore through her mind. He would kill them both.

The moon rose, and she peered through the darkness, watching him pace across the rocky platform like a madman, brandishing the pistol that glinted in the moonlight and muttering obscenities into the darkness. Kate's mind was numb with fear.

Time seemed eternal, and her heart rose to her aching throat, thinking Adam must have come by now. Yet how would he escape the hospital without being detained? Minutes seemed like hours, and she'd heard no sound but the gravel crunching beneath Lionel Valenti's feet.

Rugged stone jutted beneath her, and with her hands tied behind her back, Kate labored to fray the rope, rubbing her sore wrists against the jagged rocks. If she could free her hands, she would release her feet and escape.

Desperate, she prayed to the Lord in rhythm to the cord scraping against the stone. Her wrists stung with the burn of the rope.

A fiendish laugh broke the silence. "I see him," Lionel Valenti hissed. "He's out of the car. The fool turned off his headlights and forgot the dome light."

"Come this way, Montgomery," he taunted, "unless you don't want to see Kate again."

Kate screamed inside her head, *Go back, Adam. He won't let me go. We'll both die.*

While the madman paced, she quickened her work on the rope. A few strands gave. She wouldn't stop. She had to warn Adam that Lionel Valenti had a gun.

Sam headed along Highway 24, his ear tuned to the police dispatch. Adam's car had been spotted heading west. Sam tried to imagine the destination. Pikes Peak? No. Someplace closer with good cover. Maybe an elevated vantage point.

Earlier, when he'd asked Adam the question about which entry the doctors used at the clinic, he knew he'd found a glitch in Valenti's story. After rehashing his notes, the puzzle fell into place. The more he reviewed the facts, the more he was certain that Valenti was the culprit. Sam had called Travis and learned that barbiturates had been stolen from another hospital where Valenti had worked. That clinched it.

Drugs. The word sent an icy shiver down Sam's back. It destroyed lives. It tore apart families. It disrupted communities. One day, he prayed, Colorado Springs would be free from the growing problem.

His thoughts darted back to Adam. Ahead, a billboard stood above the landscape. Garden of the Gods. Success prickled through his chest. Yes. That had to be it. Were other squad cars on Adam's trail? He hadn't heard a recent report. He hit the radio dispatch button.

Adam crouched beside his car. He wanted to kick himself for forgetting the dome light. It spotlighted him when he climbed out, leaving no hope of surprising Valenti. Cutting the silence, he heard Valenti's laugh, assuring Adam that the man had spotted him.

He crouched low and squinted into the darkness. Boulders jutted from the outcropping of White Rock where he knew Kate must be hidden. But which boulder? Which way should he head? If she would only call out, even once…but Valenti might retaliate and harm her.

Adam drew back, protected by the vehicle, and peered above him. The moonlight glinted off something shiny. Metal? A weapon? His heart faltered. A gun? He still couldn't accept the image of the doctor falling into this pit of desperation and despair.

Drawing courage from deep inside, Adam raised his voice. "Valenti, I need to know Kate is all right."

Valenti laughed.

Silence.

"I know it's you, Lionel." Fear rushed along Adam's limbs. "You're a surgeon, man. A respected doctor. Why in the name of the good earth are you doing this?" The question was empty. Adam knew why.

Silence.

Adam wiped the perspiration from his face as he swept aside his fear. "I'm not moving until I know Kate is okay."

He listened again.

Night sounds magnified around him, then ahead on the rocks, loose gravel shifted and rolled along the sandstone. Had Valenti decided to come down the rock after him? Had he assaulted Kate? Adam's chest tightened until he couldn't breathe.

"I'm okay," Kate called, the last word muffled by Valenti's hand or a gag.

Adam's spirit rose. Kate was alive.

In the moon's dim reflection, Adam spotted a large boulder and sensed Kate's voice had come from that direction.

In a crouched position, his weakened legs buckled beneath the stress. He clung to the wheel well, waiting for a chance to dart into the underbrush and head toward the rock.

His prayer flew into the dark sky as he stayed low and made a dash for safety.

A shot rang out, its ping echoing against the high rock walls beside him. His lungs ached with fear, but he had no choice. Kate was in danger. He had to save her.

Kate in danger. An image flashed before his eyes. His unconscious dreams rose in his mind. He'd strug-

gled to save Kate from evil. Had the Lord been warning him? An image flickered through his mind—Valenti's startled face in the dispensary. Confusion and
relief bound him for a moment. The veil of his amnesia had shifted. He'd begun to remember.

Adam paused, panting with trepidation. He hunched
in the brush, keeping his head low and his legs stooped
as he crept toward the towering rock. The sounds of
Valenti's agitation had increased, but if Adam hurried,
his movements would alert Valenti.

As he shifted forward, a shadow fell across the
brush. Terror gripped Adam. He looked toward the
outcropping. Valenti was nowhere in sight.

Kate's ears rang with the blast of the weapon. Terror knotted her chest. She struggled for breath.

Her raw and aching wrists scraped against the rocks
as she felt more strands fray. In fevered desperation, she
wriggled her hands until the hemp parted, freeing her.

She tore off the duct tape, her mouth smarting with
release. Her aching fingers worked at the knots around
her ankles. Lionel Valenti had grown quiet, and she
feared what he might be planning. Had he gone down
to seek Adam, or was he shifting to a new location?

Kate feared calling out. She pressed her lips together, holding back the cries that raged inside her.

Another shot cut through the air.

Kate cringed against the boulder while her last fer-
vent attempt released her legs. She tried to gauge
where the madman had gone. Despite the darkness,
she spotted his silhouette on a higher elevation
shielded by a small boulder.

He shifted, and Kate knew she had to move now.

* * *

Sam's car skidded as he made the turn onto Ridge Road. He had been right about the location. Officers had called in verifying that Adam had turned into the park from another road. Sam had taken the shortest route.

When Sam reached Gateway Trail Road on the Juniper Way Loop, he pulled to the side where officers had gathered. He'd received word that White Rock appeared to be Valenti's rendezvous. Now under cover of darkness, Sam had directed them to make their way along Gateway Trail on foot, then circle the rock from all directions.

Hand on his gun, Sam followed the trail until the white-colored rock glinted in the moonlight. He cut through the brush and hid in the shadows, waiting for Valenti to make a move.

He wanted Valenti, but Kate slowed his progress. The officers couldn't act until they knew where she was…if she was still alive. The possibility kicked him in the gut.

Adam shrunk into the brush, his heart thundering. A twig snapped, undergrowth rustled, and he knew it was the end. *Be with Kate, Lord.* His words ascended while he waited for death.

But the steps faded, and in the darkness, he realized the intruder was not Valenti, but a police officer kneeling in the thicket, his gun aimed toward the mouth of the white rock cave.

Adam eased onto the rocky base of the formation. Weakness assailed him, but he edged forward, his feet slipping against the stone, his hands scraping against the loose gravel as he climbed and slithered upward.

His spirit soared, realizing help had reached him. Help he hadn't ask for, but help the Lord had sent his way. On eagles' wings, he thought. Today the eagle was God's promised protection in the human form. Sam? His friend's image filled him.

A raised piece of rock jutted farther up. If he could reach there, Adam hoped he could signal to Kate. He prayed as he crept upward.

Kate cowered against the rock. Had Adam been shot? She heard nothing. To her left, loose gravel rolled against the stone. Was it Lionel Valenti? He'd vanished from her sight again. He could be anywhere.

Dear Lord, be with me.

Creeping away from the boulder, Kate looked to her left. Could she make it to the lower rock without him seeing her?

As she calculated the distance, a shadow shifted near the boulder. A scream caught in her throat. She peered toward the silhouette. Recognizing the familiar physique, her spirit rejoiced.

Adam.

It was now or never.

Kate crouched, then began sprinting across the outcropping.

Spotlights glared from below, the light giving away her attempt to escape.

A bullet split the air.

Hot pain assailed her.

Sam halted, hearing the shot. He narrowed his eyes toward the ping. The large boulder. Valenti had shot in that direction, meaning someone was there. Kate? Adam? He didn't know for sure, but he moved in. An officer's shot rang out. In the glaring light, he saw Valenti duck and drop his weapon. Officers swarmed upward. They'd cornered him, and all Sam could do was pray Valenti's bullet had missed its mark.

Adam reached out and yanked Kate behind the rock as she crumpled to the ground. In the darkness, he searched for a wound. Chaos overwhelmed him. Police megaphones called for Valenti to surrender. A shot blasted, ricocheting off the stone wall nearby.

Metal clattered on the stone as confusion resounded from below. He could hear voices yelling instruction.

Not certain what had happened, Adam stayed low, cradling Kate in his arms, tears stinging his eyes.

Her moan wrung his heart, and he rested his head against her hair. "Hang on, Kate."

Footsteps clattered around him. Gravel rolled and shifted. Voices grew nearer as silhouettes appeared against the moon. Adam stayed on the ground, rocking Kate in his arms. She lay still and silent, and fear wracked his body.

A silhouette passed by, then halted and shifted backward. A shadow blocked the moonlight, and Adam lifted his head, perspiration stinging his eyes. "Sam?"

His friend crouched beside him. "Are you all right?"

"Kate's been shot."

Sam gripped his shoulder, then let go and hurried away, his voice ringing with orders.

Adam felt Kate's warm blood seep through the front of his shirt.

A siren wailed in the distance.

Chapter Eighteen

Kate pulled herself from the fog of sleep. Her eyes fluttered, and she recognized a flash of cream-colored walls. Vance Memorial Hospital.

Struggling to awaken, memory took her back to the dark hillside. The sting of the bullet, then blackness was the last she remembered. But the familiar walls assured her she had survived the evil that had stirred Lionel Valenti to madness.

Within the cozy haze of waking, a murmur reached her ears. She shifted her head and lifted her eyelids enough to catch a glimpse of Adam, sitting nearby, his eyes cast downward and his hands folded in prayer. His words washed over her like sweet nectar, and she closed her eyes again to listen.

"Lord," Adam prayed, "keep Kate in Your care. Give her a speedy recovery. I have so much to say…so much to do to make amends…things I should have done long ago. She means more to me than life itself, and I want to tell her. Father, You know my weakness. I lost my way, but You found me. I promise that I will keep Your Word in my mind and heart...."

His litany continued, and Kate's memory surged back to the stained-glass window of the Good Shepherd Christian Church. Adam's words struck her. *I lost my way, but You found me.* Her heart rejoiced at God's tremendous love. *Jesus never gives up on us,* Kate thought. *He is the way.*

Adam's words settled over her. He truly loved her. She realized it for the first time. This hadn't been a game. He hadn't been stringing her along to avoid boredom. He cared about her...as much as life itself. The beauty of the meaning nestled in her heart. She'd never thought she would hear those words.

Kate moved to alert Adam that she was awake. His gaze snapped toward the bed while his fingers unwound, and he reached for her.

"Kate." He rose and stood over her. "How are you?" His misty gaze caressed her face. Tears. Tears for her. Her heart melted, appreciating the gift.

"I'm alive," she said, thanking God for His protection and love. Her own eyes searched Adam's body, looking for a bandage or wound. She saw none. "Are *you* all right?"

His smile warmed her. "You're the one in the bed this time, not me."

"You weren't hurt?"

He leaned over and brushed his finger along her cheek. "I'm not only fine, I've been released from the hospital. They figured if I could go gallivanting all over the countryside, and do a little rock climbing, I was strong enough to get out of here."

As Kate shifted, pain shot along her arm. "What happened?" She gestured toward the soreness.

"The bullet grazed your arm. They admitted you for overnight just to keep an eye on you and give you some meds to sleep. You'll be released today, but I'll warn you. Reporters have been all around the hospital wanting to get your story of the kidnapping."

Reporters. Kidnapping. The truth fell against her chest. "I'll plead the Fifth. I don't want to remember it, Adam. I was in shock."

"At least you can remember...not like I had been."

"Had been?" She studied his face, edging upward. "Can you remember?"

He nodded. "I'm beginning to."

"Adam, I'm so relieved." She captured his hand and drew it to her lips. "And this time it's my turn to thank you for saving my life."

"Sam saved us both," he said.

"Don't get humble on me." She laughed at the paradox. "You pulled me behind the rock."

"I saw the gun," he said. "It was a gut reaction." He lowered his eyes, then lifted them with a grin. "I would have taken the bullet for you."

"I know that. I heard you praying, Adam, and I believe what you said. You would have died for me."

He reached for the chair and tugged it closer.

"Sit here," she said, patting the spot beside her.

"Are you sure I won't hurt you?"

"You'd never hurt me."

Adam eased down on the mattress and gathered her hands in his. "We have to talk."

"I'm a captive audience."

He lifted her fingers to his mouth and kissed each knuckle. "When I thought I might lose you, Kate, I could not forgive myself for letting so much time go by without facing the truth."

"Wait a minute," she said. "If I'm going to hear the truth, I want to be sitting up." She tugged at her hospital gown and shifted her legs. "Can you hand me something to throw over my shoulders?"

Adam rose and strode to the closet. He pulled out a clean hospital gown and handed it to Kate. She draped it over her shoulders and asked him to boost her.

Her head spun a moment while she gathered her bearings. When the room had stilled, she swung her legs over the edge and adjusted her robe. "I see what you mean about these gowns."

He chuckled, remembering his own plight. Adam lowered himself into the chair, his gaze riveted to hers. "Ready?"

"Ready for what?"

His eyes sparked with disappointment. "I want to tell you the truth."

She loved the look on his face, the lack of arrogance and self-importance. In their place, she saw love in his eyes. This time she reached for his hand and held it in hers. "I can't wait to hear the truth."

"I love you, Kate, with all my heart. I cherish every moment we've spent together. I've always wondered what it meant when we talk about God's plan. Although I've been raised a Christian, I couldn't understand how God allows bad things to happen to people who are trying to do their best."

Kate longed to respond, to kiss his lips, but she harnessed the words and listened.

"Now, I understand. I wasn't doing my best, at all. I was taking credit for God's gifts to me. But the Lord didn't turn his back. He allowed me to face danger and death so that I could see the truth about myself."

With his free hand, he touched her chin, his gaze looking into her soul. "I was afraid to love because I was afraid to be vulnerable. The Lord put you in my path…you with your spunky ways and your strong faith. God made it all possible. I cherish you, Kate."

His loving words pressed against her heart, and she knew she owed him the truth. "I love you, but I've been afraid."

"Afraid?"

"Afraid to let you know who I really am. I didn't want you to pity me or reject me because of my past. I didn't have enough faith to trust God to make things right. So you see, my faith wasn't strong at all."

Adam shook his head, but she went on. "I want to tell you about me, Adam, from the very beginning."

Kate's hands trembled against his as she told him the story of her life—the poverty, the hunger, the homeless shelters and loneliness.

He never wavered. His eyes searched hers with so much love she could barely contain the joy. When she'd finished, Adam rose and drew her upward.

Her legs wobbled as she stood, but Adam's strong arms held her fast. "I knew a little of your background, Kate, and I never batted an eye when I heard it the first time, and I can't believe this is what kept us apart."

"What do you mean?" She felt a frown settle on her face.

"One afternoon when my mother dropped by, she gave me a real pitch for you. She told me how wonderful you are and what a good Christian wife you'd be. Somewhere in our conversation, she hinted that you'd had a difficult life, but she said that she'd reassured you it wouldn't make a bit of difference. She was right on the mark. It doesn't."

Tears blurred Kate's eyes. "You didn't care?"

"I cared. I cared because of the difficulty you'd faced for so long, and I cared because I knew you had been hurt in the past and you hadn't told me. I could only pray that you would. Mom didn't give me the details. She's a meddler of sorts, but she respected your confidence in her. Like she tends to do, she warned me, but knowing that I'd never let that stand in my way to love."

"Does she know that you love me?"

"She knew before I did."

His arms drew her closer, and his mouth touched hers, so warm and sweet, so inviting. Her weak legs teetered, but her confidence was strong with the joy of giving her heart to the man that God had meant for her.

He eased away, his words brushing her lips. "I promise to love you always, Kate, my angel."

"I promise to make you stick to it," she said, reaching on tiptoe to capture his mouth. She held her wounded arm against her, and embraced his neck with the other while her fingers played in his dark locks. The joy to touch and taste the man of her dreams wrapped around her heart.

Thank You, Lord, she prayed. *Your love never fails.*

* * *

Adam looked up when Colleen slipped into Kate's room. "Here are your clothes. I hope I remembered everything." She set a plastic bag on the bed. "I'd better warn you. The place is surrounded with reporters."

"I know," Adam said. "I saw them earlier."

"But now they're at your town house, and Mom called to tell me TV station trucks are hanging around their place."

He slapped his hand against the nightstand and rose. "Kate's not ready for all this."

"I can handle it, Adam. I suppose I have to." Her face paled, and she clutched the bag Colleen had brought. "I just wish I had a moment to think…to get some air before I face them."

"How can we get out of here without being seen?" Adam asked.

"My car is in the parking garage. If we use the service elevator all the way down, I'll drive your car out. They're probably looking for that." Colleen chuckled. "You can take my SUV. There's a baseball cap on the back seat. Put it on. Go for a ride or something. If it gets dark, maybe they'll give up and leave."

"Good plan," Adam said. "You up for it, Kate?"

"After yesterday, I'm up for anything." She rose again, teetering for a moment, then grasped the clothing and headed for the bathroom.

Adam exchanged keys with Colleen. "When Kate's ready, you go ahead and turn right out of the parking area. I hope some will follow. We'll head left. I'll call you later."

Colleen grinned. "Did I mention I expect an exclusive for this little venture?"

"You got it," he said, giving her a quick hug.

When Kate was ready to leave, Adam found a wheelchair—hospital orders—and took her down the service elevator to the parking structure. Once settled in the SUV with his hair covered by Colleen's cap, they waited until she vanished through the exit, then followed.

As Adam had hoped, no one spotted them, and he pulled off the cap, then turned left and headed to the highway. At Kate's request, he rolled down the windows, letting the wind whip through their hair.

"I need fresh air," she'd said. "I want the stench of Valenti's madness out of my senses."

The afternoon sun had lowered in the sky, its glare spreading along the highway. The Saturday traffic was tolerable, and Adam's heart lurched when they passed the turnoff for Garden of the Gods.

"Where are we headed?" Kate asked.

Adam had no destination in mind, but as he drove through Manitou Springs, Pikes Peak rose in the distance, the lowering sun turning the top to glowing silver. "I'm taking you to the top of the world."

She gave him a questioning look but didn't ask.

Outside the town of Cascade, Adam turned onto Pikes Peak Highway and began the climb.

"Pikes Peak?" Kate asked, looking dubïous.

"Fresh air, awesome panorama and a little closer to God. You can't ask for anything better."

"I guess you're right," she said, reaching over to squeeze his hand.

The nineteen-mile ride took them to the summit, and at the top, they climbed out and stood looking out across the amazing landscape. Colorado Springs appeared as a miniature Christmas village from their height of over fourteen thousand feet—innocent and inviting.

Kate looked out on the picturesque scene. "The altitude takes my breath away."

"No, it's me, Kate," Adam said with a teasing grin.

She grinned as a shiver coursed her body.

Adam nestled her against him as the same chill penetrated his summer clothing. His thoughts turned serious. "Our lives seem so small when we look down from here."

"Small, but we are significant. We're God's children."

He drew her closer, putting his hand against her elbow so as not to jiggle her wounded arm. He admired Kate's spiritual strength. One day, he prayed he'd have a similar grasp of God's Word, but he had a long way to go.

"I've been thinking," he said, "and this vista makes it even clearer. I know that God brought us together for a purpose, and I know He's guided my thinking. I want to go back to Doctors Without Borders. I believe it's God's mission for me to head an organization like that, and you're partially to blame." He kissed the tip of her nose. "My faith has strengthened because of you."

She lowered her head. "Don't give me credit. God did all the work." She rebounded. "But I'd love to go back...anywhere I'm needed."

He kissed her hair, realizing how Kate's difficult life had prepared her for the arduous work. "Through this ordeal, I've made a promise to God that I'll do what I can to expand my missionary involvement, in Doctors Without Borders or wherever I'm called, and I promised Him to stay close to His teachings."

"That's why I love you so much," Kate said, her smile warming the chill from his body.

As the sun pressed against the distant mountains and spread its coral hues across the earth, Kate shivered again.

"I cherish you," Adam said. The summit wind grew colder and he released her and steered her toward the car. "Let's get in. It's warmer."

When they were settled inside, Adam started the engine. "We can stop in Cascade or Manitou Springs for dinner. Then I want to stop by my folks'."

"I'd like that," Kate said.

Before he shifted into gear, he opened Colleen's glove box and checked inside, then scanned the floor until he spotted something he could use. He grinned at his plan.

"Kate," he said, shifting to look at her, "I hope you realize I'm talking about marriage. I want to marry you. I want you to be part of my life and to share my hopes and dreams."

She slid her hand into his. "You're everything I've dreamed of and more."

"I haven't had an opportunity to buy you a ring, but I want to make this official." He dangled a rubber band in front of her. "Kate, will you marry me?"

"I will," she said, a silly grin settling on her face

as she stared at the office supply suspended from his finger.

He took the symbol and wound it around her ring finger. "I love you, now and forever."

She didn't answer but raised her lips to his. His mouth met hers, and at the top of his world, he tasted her precious love.

Chapter Nineteen

A week later, the Broadmoor Hotel ballroom overflowed with friends and family. Kate stood beside Adam and looked at the crowd that Liza had said would be a small group of family and friends. Kate figured Adam either had a huge family or the Montgomerys had a city's worth of friends.

She'd smiled and greeted people until her hand was sore, making her grateful her left arm had received the wound. Though it was healing, the soreness remained. Adam told her he knew a good plastic surgeon who could repair her scar if she wanted. She'd thought about keeping it just to remind her of the Lord's love and mercy.

As Adam linked his hand in hers, she became aware again of the lovely oval diamond on her finger. Its colors glinted in the light from the crystal chandeliers that hung above them. She'd almost hated to give up the rubber band and had placed it in a special spot as a remembrance. Adam laughed at her sentimentality.

Her gaze drifted over the crowd. Most people were strangers but among them she saw Colleen, Jake and Sam, of course. Aunt Fiona's red hair bounced among the guests. With so many family members, she would take forever to learn their names.

She saw Sam coming her way. Today his look had softened.

"Congratulations," he said to Adam. "And the best to you, Kate."

Adam clasped Sam's shoulder. "Thanks, and I haven't had time to thank you. If you hadn't arrived, we'd both be dead."

Sam shrugged. "I wish you had given me a clue. Valenti called while I was in your room, didn't he?"

No sense in covering now, Adam thought, as the horrible telephone call struck his thoughts. "You're right, but he threatened to kill Kate if he saw police…and I guess I didn't trust you. I'm sorry."

"I understand," Sam said, "but it was stupid. Anyway, it worked out, and that's all that's important." He shoved his hand into his pocket. "So when's the big day?"

Adam looked at Kate, and she gave him an approving nod. "Soon. Another month. Something small. Kate and I are anxious to get on with our lives. We waited too long to waste any more time."

"I can't blame you," Sam said, then used his shoulder to gesture toward Adam's parents, "but are your folks going to settle for a small wedding?"

Adam laughed. "Sure." He motioned to the crowd. "This is their version of a small engagement party."

Kate's eyes widened. "Really, Adam? Since I have no family, I figured our wedding…" Her voice faded.

Sam motioned to the guests. "This is your family now, Kate. You'll have to take them or leave them."

She eyed the crowd, and her frown turned to a smile. "Guess I'll take them."

"You'll be at the wedding, I hope," Adam said, looking into his friend's eyes and seeing an approving smile.

"As they say, I wouldn't miss it for the world."

As Sam said goodbye, Adam spotted his father heading toward the microphone, a glass of sparkling cider in his hand. Adam knew what that meant.

The microphone gave a thud as Frank stepped into place. Adam watched all eyes turn toward his father. He gave the mike a tap and lifted his glass. "Tonight is an amazing evening for Liza and me and we're grateful that so many family and friends were able to join us on such short notice. We're here to celebrate the engagement of our son, Adam, and his delightful fiancée Kate, but we also want to take this time to thank the Lord for His loving protection."

As eyes turned toward them, Adam drew Kate closer to his side, recalling how many times he'd thanked the Lord in the past few days.

"We don't want to dwell on the disturbing incident of last week. Instead I want to make a toast to my son and my soon-to-be daughter-in-law. Liza and I have been married for nearly thirty-seven years. I can only speak for myself, but I am grateful every day that the Lord led me to this wonderful woman."

The crowd applauded, and Adam watched his mother brush away Frank's comment while her face beamed with his words.

"Adam and Kate, I want to leave you with a few

words to think about—words your mother and I lived by. They're not mine, but they belong to Someone even greater than the mayor of Colorado Springs.''

Titters skittered through the crowd.

''This comes from First Corinthians thirteen.''

The laughter quieted. Adam looked with pride at his father, then gazed at Kate. Her eyes brimmed with tears. He slid his arm around her back and drew her closer.

Frank looked at Adam and Kate. '''Love is patient and kind. It's not rude or self-seeking. Love doesn't delight in evil but rejoices in truth. It always protects, always trusts, always hopes, always perseveres. Love never fails. Now these three remain: faith, hope and love. But the greatest of these is love.''' He lifted his glass. ''Adam and Kate, your mother and I wish you many years of happiness, and most of all, we wish you God's blessings.''

Voices echoed in agreement. Glasses were raised and the cider was sipped to wish them God's grace.

''How about kissing your lovely fiancée?'' a voice rang out. Others joined in the chant.

Adam captured Kate's gaze. Her eyes sparkled brighter than the diamond he'd placed on her finger earlier that day. ''I love you, Kate. I'll cherish you for the rest of my days.''

''Promise?'' she said. ''Because I love you, too, Adam, more than I can ever say.''

''Promise,'' he said. ''Forever.''

In front of God and all the witnesses, Adam lowered his mouth to the most beautiful woman in the world. His angel. His Kate.

* * * * *

A little girl is missing and it's up
to Samuel Vance to locate her,
in FINDING AMY,
coming only to Love Inspired
in August 2004.
And now for a sneak preview,
please turn the page.

Chapter One

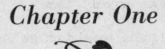

Love songs crooned for Dr. Adam Montgomery and Kate Darling, the couple whose engagement sparked the laughter and happiness tonight. After arresting Dr. Lionel Valenti for shooting Adam in Venezuela and kidnapping and assaulting Kate, Samuel Vance should have been elated. Unfortunately, Valenti hadn't been as cooperative as they'd hoped he would be during the questioning. Sam needed something more than suspicion to tie Valenti to the Diablo crime syndicate. Tension in the division was at a peak. After almost a week, neither Sam nor any of the other top-notch interrogators had gotten the doctor to crack.

Sam heard Jessica laugh. The kind of party-girl giggle that spread like a virus. He watched the man beside her turn to putty.

"You're looking awfully cranky tonight," his ex-sister-in-law teased. Emily followed his gaze and smiled softly. "Interesting view, isn't it?"

He shrugged, dismissing her baited question. "Interesting to who?"

She nudged him. "I have news for you, Samuel, you're not that discreet. Face it, you Vance men don't look if you don't like the woman."

He glanced back at Jessica, angry that Emily had caught him. He could try to deny Emily's accusation, but he'd never succeed. "There's an exception to every rule."

Emily's laughter bounced off the Colonial pane windows surrounding the Broadmoor Hotel ballroom and practically shattered the crystal chandelier. Sam felt as if a spotlight had just turned on them. His dad glanced over and headed toward him and Emily.

Sam didn't want to talk business right now. Especially not when his parents were together. He had questions for his father that couldn't be asked—let alone answered—in public. "Now look what you've done," he said, razzing Emily. He scoped out their proximity to the exits. "It's too far to the door to escape."

"Don't be silly. Why would you want to do that? Look, your mom and dad are bringing the woman with them." Emily complimented his parents, impressed that they looked so young and in love.

Sam turned away from the oncoming trio, intending to take the shortest route out of the ballroom. Leave it to an engagement to put his mother in matchmaker mode. She and Mrs. Montgomery were both anxious for their families to grow. "I'm leaving. Care to join me?"

Emily followed. "Sam, what has gotten into you?"

"Let's just say it's business related. And the last thing I want to talk about tonight is work."

"You and your father have to learn to communicate now that he's retired, Sam. He's home. Make the best of it."

"He's here, all right. In my face. On the job and off." *Just like Jessica Mathers.*

Sam looked over his shoulder, relieved to find his mother introducing his dad and Jessica to one of her bridge club buddies. He took Emily by the elbow and zigzagged through the elegant surroundings where all of Colorado Springs' socialites and a few working stiffs like himself gathered in party attire. Sam removed his sport coat, hoping to cool off outside.

Emily simply waited for further explanation.

Sam grumbled about the impromptu celebration. "I'm not much for these shindigs."

Emily gave him a dirty look, even as he opened the door to the terrace for her.

"Samuel Vance. You should be happy for them." Emily scolded him like only a "sister" could.

Unsuccessful at ignoring her scowl, he conceded. "I am happy. Believe me. I'm happier than anyone in this city that Adam and Kate are still here to celebrate."

"I hear the wedding's at the end of the month. Sounds like they're anxious to return to the clinic in Santa Maria de Flores. Now can you make a little better attempt to enjoy yourself?"

He shook his head. "My mood has nothing to do with the party. I told you that. And I'd rather drop the subject."

As if she knew better than to try to intervene

between the Vance men, Emily remained silent. Sam looked to the heavens and said a prayer. The August sun dangled above Pikes Peak, promising a colorful sunset. That alone assured Sam that God was in control, tonight and every night.

It suddenly dawned on Sam that Emily's silence might have more to do with her divorce from his brother than anything else. Stress built up inside law-enforcement personnel—issues that couldn't be shared, even with loved ones. Sometimes especially because they were loved ones. "I'm sorry, Emily, I shouldn't have said anything."

"That part of the Vance life just never goes away, does it? Everything's top secret."

Something in her comment sounded like a freshly opened wound. "You heard from Peter?"

Emily leaned against the planter filled with bright red geraniums and tiny white flowers. Her voice softened. "No, I gave up on that long ago. You don't expect anything from an undercover agent. That way you're not disappointed."

"Even a do-better like you won't make it to heaven telling lies like that, Doc." He reached out and offered a brotherly hug. "You have every right to be disappointed. We just have to trust God is watching over Peter, wherever he's at."

Dear Reader,

I hope you enjoyed the first story of the series FAITH ON THE LINE. Though Adam's and Kate's struggles may be a little different from our own, many of us cling to our flaws and fears and let them control our lives. Kate held on to her past, ashamed of what people might think. Adam used his aloofness and arrogance to shield him from relationships.

But the most important lesson in *Adam's Promise* is what God will do for us if we let Him. He will give us strength and protection, and Jesus, the Good Shepherd, will find us when we stray and return us safely to the fold.

If flaws and griefs of the past hold you in bondage, remember that Jesus is the Way and "God works for the good of those who love Him."

Next month look for Carol Steward's *Finding Amy*, in the continuing saga of FAITH ON THE LINE. You'll spend more time with the Montgomery and Vance families as they fight to rid Colorado Springs of crime.

Thanks for reading Steeple Hill Love Inspired. May God send you His richest blessings.

Gail Gaymer Martin

AUTUMN PROMISES

BY

KATE WELSH

Evan Alton had cut himself off from most of the world, except his children, for years. But when his twin grandbabies needed him, the rancher would do anything, even allow the infuriating Meg Taggert to stay on the ranch to help. Yet caring for the twins brought him and Meg close, and made Evan feel alive for the first time in years. Perhaps the babies weren't the only ones Meg was sent to help....

Don't miss

AUTUMN PROMISES

On sale August 2004

Available at your favorite retail outlet.

Take 2 inspirational love stories FREE!

PLUS get a FREE surprise gift!

Mail to Steeple Hill Reader Service™

In U.S.
3010 Walden Ave.
P.O. Box 1867
Buffalo, NY 14240-1867

In Canada
P.O. Box 609
Fort Erie, Ontario
L2A 5X3

YES! Please send me 2 free Love Inspired® novels and my free surprise gift. After receiving them, if I don't wish to receive anymore, I can return the shipping statement marked cancel. If I don't cancel, I will receive 4 brand-new novels every month, before they're available in stores! Bill me at the low price of $4.24 each in the U.S. and $4.74 each in Canada, plus 25¢ shipping and handling and applicable sales tax, if any*. That's the complete price and a savings of over 10% off the cover prices—quite a bargain! I understand that accepting the books and gift places me under no obligation ever to buy any books. I can always return a shipment and cancel at any time. Even if I never buy another book from Steeple Hill, the 2 free books and the surprise gift are mine to keep forever.

113 IDN DZ9M
313 IDN DZ9N

Name	(PLEASE PRINT)	
Address	Apt. No.	
City	State/Prov.	Zip/Postal Code